Aaron is behaving like a brat, and he knows it. He can't help how he feels, though—at only nineteen, his life is overwhelming. He's the only harpy-Krsnik hybrid of his age, and it makes him feel like a freak. The fact that he has no idea what to do with his life doesn't help. His dads won't let him become a vampire hunter, but Aaron is old enough to make these decisions for himself.

Right?

James is working as an apprentice baker, and he loves it. His life is entrenched in Gillham, and he's not planning on ever moving. He's jealous of his brother, who at twenty, is already living with his mate, but he's not in a rush.

Then James meets his mate, and Aaron flies away—talk about being rejected. James has no intention of begging Aaron to accept him, even though he doesn't want to give up this opportunity. Will Aaron finally grow up, at least enough to see that his life is not the disaster he feels it is? And will James have the patience to wait for him?

Aaron

ISBN: 978-1-4874-3176-1
Cover art by Angela Waters

Published by eXtasy Books Inc or
Devine Destinies, an imprint of eXtasy Books Inc

Look for us online at:
www.eXtasybooks.com or www.devinedestinies.com

Aaron
Wyoming Shifters: 12 Years Later 10

By

Catherine Lievens

CHAPTER ONE

Aaron was hiding. He needed to make sure no one found him because he would have to do something he didn't want if they did.

Play with his siblings.

He sighed and glared at his bedroom door. He was nineteen. He shouldn't have to play with Hazel and Matthew, but he already knew that his fathers would ask him to if they found out he was here. He should have left when he'd had the opportunity, but Matthew had been having a meltdown in the hallway, and Aaron had retreated to his bedroom.

And now he was stuck.

He eyed the window. Maybe he wasn't as stuck as he thought. He didn't like shifting, but for this, he would.

"Aaron?" one of his fathers called out. Aaron was pretty sure it was Emery, but he couldn't tell through the closed bedroom door.

This was it. They were going to check his bedroom, and they would find out he was there. If Aaron wanted out, he needed to do something *now*.

He got to his feet, shrugged off his t-shirt, and shifted.

His father always became massive when he shifted into his harpy form, but Aaron wasn't like him. Everyone kept telling him it would change when he grew up, but he was already nineteen, and there was no way he would become as muscular as his father when he shifted. It didn't make sense that Troy looked that way, either. Aaron supposed his dad looked okay, but he had a bit of a stomach, and he was on the out of shape side when he was human. How could he be so muscled in his harpy form?

Aaron looked down at himself. He was skinny, just like his other dad. There were muscles there, but not too many, which made him scowl again.

"Aaron? Are you in your bedroom?"

Aaron opened the window and climbed onto the sill. He didn't look back as he threw himself down.

He opened his wings, and the wind caught them. He rose, but it only took a few flaps to get him safely on the ground under his window. From there, he could hear his bedroom door open after a knock, and he hurriedly pressed himself against the wall so that even if his father looked down, he wouldn't see him. He shifted and shivered, knowing his dad would know what he'd done. There was no way he would have opened his bedroom window otherwise.

Aaron heard a noise above him, and he knew his dad was leaning out the window. He didn't say anything, and Aaron didn't dare move. He would hear enough about this later when he went back home. When he heard the window close, he breathed out and put his t-shirt back on. He probably should have thought better about this. He wasn't sure where to go. It was too late to head to Whitedell, and while he did have friends here at the mansion, the whole place was busy and noisy, just as much as his parents' private rooms. Aaron's entire life was busy and loud, which was why he'd been hiding.

With a sigh, he walked around the house to the kitchen. His dads would find him soon enough, but he supposed he could take advantage of the hour or so it would take them to calm down the kids and look for him.

The sliding doors of the kitchen were closed but not locked. Aaron opened them and stepped in, the smell of food wrapping around him and making him relax, even though it was mixed with a burning smell.

He shouldn't have left, and especially not through the window. He just needed some time to himself, and he hoped his fathers would understand.

"Where did you come from?" Nysys asked. He was standing at the stove, poking at something in a pan.

Aaron wasn't sure what that something was, since it looked like a charcoal brick by now. "Outside."

Nysys looked at him and rolled his eyes. "I can see that. What were you doing outside? I thought you were upstairs."

"You thought wrong. Did you want something?"

Nysys arched a brow. "When did you become so mouthy?" He raised a hand. "Wait. Don't tell me. You were always mouthy. I wonder who you took that from? Neither of your fathers are like that."

"Are you saying my dad cheated on my father?"

Nysys' eyes went wide. "How did you get that from what I just said? Of course not. Neither of them would do something like that. They're mates."

It was Aaron's turn to roll his eyes. "Being mates doesn't mean you don't cheat."

"It does in this pride, and they love each other too much to even think about doing something like that. Now, did *you* need anything? I'm cooking dinner, and it should be ready soon."

Aaron looked at the pan again. "I'm going to go upstairs. I'm sure my dads are looking for me."

"I thought you were running away from them."

"I never said I was running away."

"You didn't have to. You looked like someone was hunting you when you walked in."

"No one's hunting me."

"Not even Hazel?"

Aaron sighed. "I love her."

"But she's eight, and she wants to spend all of her time with her big brother. I know you don't like it, but she's not doing it to bother you."

Aaron knew that, but it didn't make it easier to accept. He'd been an only child for fifteen years, then suddenly, in less than a year, he'd found himself with two siblings. Hazel had been adopted, but it didn't change anything. She was part of their family, and while Aaron loved her and Matthew, he needed space.

"There you are," a voice said from the entrance of the kitchen.

Aaron groaned and looked at his father. "You were looking for me?"

Emery rolled his eyes. "You know I was. Isn't that why you jumped out the window?"

Nysys made a strangled sound, but thankfully, he didn't say anything. Aaron ignored him. "I didn't jump out the window."

"Really? Because that's what Troy told me."

"He wasn't there. He can't know what I did."

Emery shook his head. "All right. Well, you're nineteen, so I suppose I can't forbid you to jump out your bedroom window. Just make sure you don't hurt yourself, okay?"

Aaron felt a stab of guilt in his chest. He knew his fathers loved him, and so did Matthew and Hazel. But sometimes, they were so *much*. "Did you need me?"

"Not really, not if you don't want to take care of your siblings for a bit."

"I'd like to talk to you."

Emery rubbed his face. "Sure. We can do that as soon as the kids are in bed. Are you coming upstairs for dinner?"

"You're not eating with the others?"

"Matthew is having a rough night, so probably not."

Matthew often had rough nights, and while Aaron tried

not to be bitter, he couldn't help it. His fathers devoted most of their time to his siblings, and it made him angry. "I think I'm going to go out."

"Out where?"

"You just said I'm nineteen. I don't have to tell you where I'm going."

His father looked at him, and Aaron waited for him to push, to demand an answer. He wouldn't have one. He didn't know where to go, but he had to get away from the house.

He felt like a child, jealous of his sister and brother. He knew why his fathers focused so much time on them. They were young, and they needed it. Aaron had been lucky that he'd had his fathers' undivided attention when he'd been growing up, but it was still hard not to have it anymore.

"All right. I'll see you later, then," his father said.

Aaron gaped as his dad turned around to leave. He couldn't believe that had just happened, although, in a way, he could.

His fathers loved him. He was sure of that. He knew that the fact that he was a weird hybrid didn't change anything for them. What *had* changed things was not being an only child anymore, and even though he loved his siblings, he also resented them.

"That could have gone better," Nysys said.

"Did you need something?" Aaron snapped.

Nysys didn't look offended. "I don't, no, but I think *you* do. Want to talk about it?"

"There's nothing to talk about."

"I'm pretty sure that's not true, but fine. We'll act as if everything is going perfectly. Want to help cook dinner?"

Aaron didn't, but it was nice to feel wanted, so he agreed.

He was one of a kind. Well, Matthew was like him, but Matthew was only four. He didn't know how bad it was to be a human, harpy, and Krsnik hybrid, and for the only people he could talk to about it to be too busy to even look at him.

Everything had been weird since Lee had met his mate. James didn't resent him for that. He was happy for his brother, but things had changed.

Lee was one year younger than James, yet there he was, living with his mate, his life under control. He worked at the shelter, and he was studying to be a vet.

What did James have to be proud of?

James knew his parents didn't care. Even though Lee had his life under control, he was only nineteen. James was twenty and still young. Besides, it wasn't like his life was a mess. He was doing pretty good, even though he wasn't in a relationship and was still living with his parents. Still, watching Lee with his mate made James feel like a child.

It made him feel like he wasn't doing enough.

"You should go to bed," his mother said. "You have to get up early tomorrow."

"I know. You don't have to remind me every night. You also don't have to wake me up anymore." She'd started that right after James began working as an apprentice at the bakery. It had been hard on her, and James was glad she'd finally listened to him and had stopped. He didn't need breakfast at three in the morning. He just needed to get up, get dressed, and head out.

"You just looked tired," his mother continued.

"That's because I am. It's getting late." He was used to going to bed around seven or eight in the evening. He had to, if he wanted to be able to wake up at three in the morning and be at the bakery in time. Lee and his mate were here for dinner, though, which meant he hadn't been able to do that today.

"You shouldn't let us stop you from going to bed," Lee

said. "We understand."

Lee's mate, Telyn, nodded. He was always quiet, but he was relaxing with their family, which was good to see. James knew Telyn's history, and he was glad he'd found a new family with them.

Even though sometimes they were all annoying as hell.

"I'm fine. I'll be going upstairs soon, but it's a family dinner. I should spend time with my family."

Lee stared at James for a while.

James suspected he could tell something was wrong, and he wasn't looking forward to his brother asking questions. He would, though. He always did.

James tried to forget about it during the rest of the evening. Telyn was quiet, as always, but James' mom made up for it. She chatted with him, trying to get answers out of him that weren't a nod and a smile. James wanted to tell her to stop, but he didn't. She wanted Telyn to feel like part of their family, and she thought she would achieve that by forcing him to talk. James could have told her it wouldn't work, although he supposed that in time, maybe it would. It wasn't like Telyn was going anywhere. For good or bad, he was part of their family now that he and Lee were together.

As soon as dinner was over, James got to his feet. He picked up his plate, but his mother stopped him. "You don't have to do that. You should go to bed."

"I'm going," James told her with a roll of his eyes. "And I'm not going to help you clean up, if that's what you're wondering. I was just going to leave my plate in the sink."

She stared at him for a moment and nodded. "All right. Have a good night."

"I will. I'll try not to wake you and Dad when I leave."

"Don't worry about us," James's father said. "It's work. We don't mind."

James was pretty sure they would if he continued waking

them up at three in the morning, but they would never say anything about it. They were happy that he had a job.

He understood where they were coming from. Lee had a job and was going to college. James had never done that, and he didn't think he wanted to. School hadn't been for him, and he doubted college would be any different.

Still, it didn't help with his feeling of inferiority when it came to Lee. It was stupid, but he couldn't help how he felt.

After saying his goodbyes, he left the dining room. He started climbing the stairs, but he wasn't surprised when he heard someone behind him. He paused when he got to the second floor so that Lee could catch up with him. "You need anything?" he asked.

Lee stared at him again.

It made James want to say something, but since his brother had followed him, he should be the one to speak first.

"What's going on?" Lee finally asked.

"Nothing. I'm going to bed because I have work early."

"That's not what I'm talking about."

"*What* are you talking about?"

"I don't know. You tell me. You've been acting weird. Is it because of Telyn? You don't like him?"

"Of course I like him. Who wouldn't?" Telyn was a demon, but no one cared. They only cared about the fact that he was Lee's mate, and more importantly, that he was a good person. His mother had made his life hell, but now, he was away from her, and he could finally live.

"What is it, then?" Lee insisted.

James sighed. "You're going to push until I tell you, aren't you?"

"I am. You know better than to try avoiding me," Lee said with a hint of humor in his voice.

James did, though. If he didn't tell Lee what was going on, Lee would continue asking about it. It would get to the point where James would snap, and then he would feel guilty. That was the last thing he needed considering how he already felt about this entire situation. "It's really nothing," he started.

"It has to be something if it makes you feel bad. I can see it. Come on, Jamesy. Tell me what's wrong. I can't help fix it if you don't."

James looked downstairs, but no one was there. He could hear the family talking in the dining room. "Shouldn't you go rescue Telyn?"

"I will as soon as we're done here. He doesn't mind me being here with you."

James was sure he didn't. He was just that kind of guy. "It's really stupid," he warned.

"I'll be the judge of that."

"It's just that sometimes when you're around, I feel like a failure."

Lee blinked. "What are you talking about?"

"You're nineteen, yet you have a job, you're going to college, and you have a mate. You live with him. You have your life under control, and you're an adult."

"So are you."

James snorted. "I still live with my parents."

"So? It doesn't mean you're not an adult or that you're not living like one. You have a job, and it's not an easy one. I wouldn't be able to wake up at three in the morning to go to work every day."

"I just work at a bakery."

"So what? It's a job. I like animals. You like baking. What's the difference?"

James supposed there wasn't one, not really. "Fine. I have a job. What about everything else, though?"

Lee shrugged. "None of that means you're not an adult. I was lucky to meet my mate when I was only nineteen, but I know most people don't. *You* didn't. It doesn't make you less of an adult. As for the fact that you still live with our parents, that doesn't, either. You're only twenty, and you're still getting used to your new job. What would you do if you lived in your own apartment? If I know you, you'd have a jumbled routine. You'd barely eat because you're so busy, and your place would be horribly messy. I think it's good that you still live at home, at least for now. But if you really don't like it, you should look for your own apartment."

He was right. No matter how all of this made James feel, he could make changes. That was what made him an adult. It was making his own decisions when it came to his life.

He knocked their shoulders together. "Thanks," he said.

Lee smiled. "You have nothing to thank me for. Now go to bed. I'll come by the bakery tomorrow morning to taste your stuff."

James laughed. "I didn't know you were so brave." But it felt good to be like this with his brother. Things were changing, but not so much that they weren't close anymore. James and Lee would always be brothers, no matter what happened in their lives.

Aaron didn't try to be quiet, even though he knew that at least Matthew would already be sleeping. Well, he hoped so. Sometimes his brother stayed up until midnight, no matter how hard their fathers tried to put him to bed.

Life had been so much easier when Aaron had been an only child.

He never told anyone about this, though. People would tell him he was acting like a child, and they would be right. He was nineteen. He was supposed to be an adult, not to need his parents anymore. It was normal for them to devote their time to his siblings. They were young, while Aaron could stand up on his own.

That didn't make him less jealous, though.

He loved his fathers, and he'd had their undivided attention for fifteen years. He'd needed it, and he still did, but now, he felt like they didn't care much anymore. When he forced himself to think about it, he knew he was an idiot, but he couldn't help how he felt. His dads never had time for him anymore, even when he asked. They also barely had the energy. He still needed them, but they didn't seem to remember he was their son.

The apartment was quiet when he got there. He held his breath as he closed the front door, listening, but no one was crying, singing, or screaming. It was strangely calm, as if something was about to happen, and he prayed it didn't.

He knew he was going to be in trouble. His dads didn't want him to jump out the window, although that was mostly because he'd broken a leg once a few years ago. He was better at it now, even though he still shifted as little as possible.

When he stepped into the living room, he found both his dads on the couch. Aaron took a moment to look at them.

They were both tired. That much was obvious. Troy was stretched out on the couch with his head on Emery's lap while Emery carded his fingers into Troy's hair. It glinted red in the light, and Aaron thought about his own red hair.

He looked like both his fathers, which was a strange mix, to say the least.

Emery looked up and smiled. "There you are," he said.

Troy twisted into a sitting position. "We were getting worried," he said. "I know you're nineteen, but you're still our son. That's never going to change, and neither is the fact that we worry if we don't know where you are."

Aaron was divided between wanting to tell them that he was an adult and that he didn't have to tell them what was going on in his life and being pleased that they obviously cared about him. It meant a lot. "I was downstairs with everyone else. I didn't go out."

Emery nodded. "Good. You said you wanted to talk to us about something. What is it?"

Aaron swallowed. He knew he had to talk to his fathers about what was next for him. He was nineteen, and he'd finished high school. He had to make decisions about his future, and he didn't know where to start. He didn't know what he wanted to be, if he wanted to go to college or find a job, or anything else.

He opened his mouth to tell them, but just then, Matthew started calling out. Aaron snapped his mouth shut and glared.

Troy sighed and got to his feet. "I'll get it. I'm sure he only wants a glass of water or something like that."

Aaron knew he had to go, but he still resented it, even though he didn't say anything. His dad already had a hard enough time. He didn't need Aaron to make it even harder.

Still, it showed him that he didn't matter as much. He knew that his fathers had to focus on his siblings because they were younger, but they barely had time for him. They loved him, and Aaron was never going to doubt that, but he needed more than love. He needed their attention. He needed them to show they cared.

"You can tell me if you want," Emery said.

Aaron flopped onto the couch. He didn't want to talk about it anymore, but he supposed he needed to ask questions if he wanted to do what he had in mind. He might not have the faintest idea of what he wanted to do as an adult, but his father had been a vampire hunter. It was in their blood, and Aaron had been playing with the idea that he could follow in his father's steps. "Tell me about your life before you met Dad."

Emery's eyebrows rose on his forehead, but he didn't ask why Aaron wanted to know. "It was hard. I didn't have a home like I do now. I barely had a family. I didn't have time for anything that wasn't hunting vampires. You already know that, though."

"Was it that bad? I know you lost your family to vampires, but you found a new one."

"And I'll always be grateful. I still miss my parents, though, and my siblings. I miss my aunts and uncles, my cousins. All of them are dead because of vampires and because we didn't stop hunting them."

"You're a Krsnik. It's your duty to hunt vampires. It's what you were born for. What *I* was born for."

Aaron had said too much. His father straightened, frowning. "What are you talking about?"

"Nothing."

"Don't lie to me, Aaron."

"I'm not lying. I was just wondering what I could do now that I'm out of high school."

"And you thought you could hunt vampires?"

"I don't know what I want to do, but I'm your son, which means that hunting vampires is in my blood. Why shouldn't I do it?"

Of course, that was the moment Troy walked back into the living room. He heard Aaron's words, and he went so pale that Aaron briefly wondered if he was going to faint. "You're not going to be a vampire hunter," Troy snapped.

Aaron glared. He'd never said he wanted to be one, but he'd been curious. Now that his fathers were forbidding him to hunt vampires, he wanted to do it more than ever. "You can't tell me what to do," he pointed out. "I'm nineteen. I'm an adult."

"Barely, and you still live under our roof. You're still our son."

"I'll always be your son. Are you going to forbid me to do things even when I'm thirty? When I'm fifty?"

Troy's face twisted, but Aaron didn't know what it meant. "I'm going to forbid you to do things until you're a hundred if they're stupid and dangerous."

Aaron shook his head. "You won't even listen to me."

"I don't need to listen to you to know what I heard. You're not going to be a vampire hunter, Aaron, not on my watch."

"You can't tell me what to do. And if living with you is a problem, I'm sure I can find an apartment in town or even in another town." He turned toward the front door. He couldn't stay here, not like this.

"Where are you going?" Emery asked.

"Away, since you don't seem to want me to live with you anymore."

"That's not what I said," Troy tried.

Aaron was angry, though. Just like always, his fathers hadn't listened. They'd jumped to conclusions, they'd forbidden him to do things, but they hadn't *listened*. Aaron wasn't surprised, but he was resentful. Was it too much to ask for his fathers to consider him a son and to act like they cared about him and his life?

He slammed the front door behind himself, but he didn't stop, not even when his fathers called for him. He knew they would try to find him, which meant he had to leave as soon as possible. He couldn't stay in the house.

There was only one place he could go, and thankfully, it would take him a while to get there, which meant he would have time to think.

James groaned when the alarm on his phone started ringing. It was ass o'clock in the morning, and like always, he had to get up and head to the bakery. Some days, he wondered if he'd made a mistake by taking this job.

He wasn't a baker, just an apprentice, which meant he had to do the grunt work. He took care of mixing batters and doughs, packaging the products, and making sure they didn't burn in the ovens. Al, his boss, was the one who had the most fun. He was a traditional man, and James wished he could be more creative, and he hoped that he would, eventually, and that he'd allow James to do more.

James loved baking. In the beginning, he'd decided to do this because he had fond memories of baking with his mom. It had been a job like any other, something to get him out of the house now that he'd graduated high school. He'd tried several other jobs before the bakery, but this was the only thing that had stuck, and he could see himself doing it in the long run.

Even though the hours were awful.

There was something about baking bread, cookies, and cakes that calmed him. Maybe Lee was right and James was already an adult, even though he didn't feel like one. He hoped that would change, eventually. He couldn't imagine himself at thirty-five or forty years old still feeling like a kid.

He pushed his sloppy hair out of his eyes as he silently walked through the house. In the beginning, his mother had woken up before him so she could get breakfast ready, but thankfully, she'd stopped. He didn't need her to wake him up anymore. He was twenty, not ten. Still, he missed their quiet moments together at three in the morning. Now that James was grown up, he didn't spend as much time with his mother as he used to, especially not in the kitchen.

Maybe being an adult wasn't that great after all.

Even though he missed his mom in the mornings, waking up this early had its perks. He liked the quiet, the stillness. It wasn't just his house, either. Pack territory was silent, as was the town, once he drove into it. The world never seemed to stop, except in these quiet hours of the morning.

The lights were already on when he got to the bakery. He wasn't surprised to see Al was already there, no doubt baking and cooking. He had a bit of a problem with insomnia, which meant that more often than not, James found him already busy when he got to work. He was going to try to send Al back to bed for at least a few hours until the shop opened, but he doubted Al would agree. He was stubborn as hell, and no matter how much James pushed, Al didn't budge, both when it came to his sleeping schedule and when it came to changing things a bit in the bakery.

James knew it was too soon. He'd only been working here for a few months, and even though he loved it, he was still learning. This wasn't his shop—it was Al's, and it had been his mother's before that. It made sense that he didn't want to change things around.

James got out of his car and locked it up. When he turned to move toward the bakery, he noticed something in the sky. He pressed his back against his car, unable to look away. For the first few moments, he had no idea what he was looking at. It was too big to be a bird, even though it had wings. He knew better than to move, even though he was tempted once he realized what was going on.

It was a man, not an angel. James knew about Aaron, so he recognized him. Aaron was a member of the Whitedell pride, but he often visited Gillham. He had friends here. James was pretty sure none of them would be awake at three in the morning, though. Besides, Aaron had landed in town, not in pack territory. It didn't look like he was here to visit Adam, but James might be wrong.

James watched as Aaron landed. He was too far away to see much of anything, especially in the darkness, but it was still impressive. If he hadn't known about Aaron, he would have thought he was in front of an angel. Aaron wasn't an angel, though. He was a harpy, which explained the wings.

They disappeared once Aaron shifted. James was curious as to how that worked, but he stayed right where he was and watched Aaron look around and cross the road to head to the park. He wanted to go and ask what was going on, but he and Aaron had never talked. Now wasn't the time to start.

Once Aaron had disappeared into the darkness, James turned to the bakery. He headed toward the back door, smiling at the scent of yeast and sugar that hit him as soon as he opened it. Sure enough, Al was there, his back to James, his hands busy. He barely turned around when he heard the door, already knowing it was James.

James didn't say anything. He went to the small break room, leaving his backpack and his jacket there. He put on a white jacket, washed his hands, and went back to the bakery's main area. "Good morning," he said.

Al grunted.

That was as much of an answer as James was going to get. He wasn't offended. Al was never talkative at three in the morning, and James didn't blame him.

"What do you want me to do?" he asked. He knew better than to start doing what he thought needed to be done. He might work here, but this was still Al's bakery, while James was only an apprentice.

"Check the bread in the oven," Al said.

James took a deep breath. His day had started, and he had to get to work.

Working in a bakery wasn't easy. James hadn't expected that when he'd first applied, only thinking about the time he'd spent in the kitchen with his mother. This was different, though. It was *harder*. James spent his days working in a hot and messy environment. Al was a good baker, but he didn't have a knack for cleaning, especially now that he had an apprentice. That left James running around cleaning counters and washing dishes. The fact that it was always hot didn't make it easier, and neither did the irregular work hours. It was hell on his social life, and he still wasn't used to it. He might like the silence that cushioned life at three in the morning, but it didn't mean he didn't wish things were different once it got to five or six in the afternoon. That was the hardest time—when James was exhausted and wanted nothing more than a shower and his bed. The fact that he had to stand on his feet for so long with little rest didn't help, but right now, he was ready to face whatever today threw at him.

As he worked, though, his thoughts went back to Aaron. What was he doing in Gillham at this hour of the night? Even if he was here to see his friends, it didn't make sense. Adam, Sterling, and Sterling's siblings were bound to be asleep. Besides, Aaron had been in town instead of pack territory, which pointed to him being here for a different reason.

Why?

James had to put Aaron out of his mind. It wasn't his business, whatever Aaron was doing here, and he needed to stay out of it. He also needed to focus on his job before he ruined a batter or burned the cupcakes Al was working on right now.

That was what being an adult meant. He had a job to do, and he was going to do it and do it well.

No matter what time it was.

Chapter Two

Aaron was too young for his body to hurt like this, but he supposed that spending the night on a park bench did that to a person.

He stretched out, wincing at the flashes of pain in his back and shoulders. He looked around, his gaze meeting the gaze of a woman walking by holding the hand of a little girl. She looked away, and Aaron realized what this had to look like. People probably thought he was homeless, and he almost bolted, because he didn't want people to pity him.

Instead, he twisted and sat up. He *wasn't* homeless, even though he'd spent the night on a bench.

It had been a stupid idea. His fathers were bound to be frantic, and Aaron would be lucky if they didn't lock him up in his bedroom once they got their hands on him. No matter how many times he repeated that he was nineteen, they weren't wrong. He was still their son, and they would make sure he was punished for this. He wouldn't blame them. He'd acted on impulse, and he should have thought better of it.

But now he was in Gillham. He'd wanted to come here to see Adam and talk to him, but he'd realized when he'd arrived that Adam was probably already asleep. He hadn't even bothered going to pack territory, just in case someone noticed him and thought they were under attack or something like that. It wouldn't be the first time, and Aaron didn't want to risk it.

He took his phone out, smiling when he saw it was nine in the morning. He had a hard time believing he'd slept that long, especially with how uncomfortable he'd been, but the flight had exhausted him. He wasn't used to flying long-distance like that. Usually he used an app to get a Nix to shimmer him around. He supposed that was one more proof he'd been stupid. At the very least, he should have shifted in his eagle form instead of the harpy one.

Adam answered after only one ring. "What the fuck is going on?"

Aaron blinked. "I don't know. What's going on?"

"Why do I have your parents calling me in the middle of the night because they can't find you?"

Dammit. Aaron had hoped his fathers would give him time. Instead, they'd already started calling around. "I'll call them," he promised.

"You better. They've been blowing up my phone, and I like to sleep." He sighed. "What's going on, Aaron?"

"Can you meet me?"

"Where?"

"The coffee shop in Gillham."

"You're in Gillham?"

"I am. I should have told my dads, but we had a fight, and I didn't think about it."

"Someday, you're going to have to start thinking. Today was not that day, but fine. I'll meet you. Give me half an hour."

"I'll be at the coffee shop. I need coffee."

"I bet you do. Don't do anything stupid."

Adam hung up, and Aaron got up from the bench. He stretched again. After last night, he was still tired and angry, but he was also relieved he'd see his friend. He didn't want to talk to his parents right now, though, so he limited himself to texting them. He made sure to tell them he was fine, that he was in Gillham, and that Adam hadn't known anything about it. He promised he would go home eventually, but he didn't say when.

He didn't want to go home. He didn't want to see his dads. He wasn't punishing them, but he needed space, and now that he'd taken it, they were pushing to talk to him when they usually didn't bother. He should have known this would happen.

He made his way to the coffee shop, ordering the strongest coffee they had and sitting at a table in the corner. He closed his eyes as he sipped, finally relaxing.

Until Adam arrived. He glared at Aaron, and Aaron knew this wasn't going to be pleasant. He squared his shoulders and waited for his friend.

Adam had been his best friend once, and Aaron supposed he still was. They'd grown up together in the Whitedell pride, but Adam was a few years older than Aaron. When he'd met his mate, he hadn't hesitated to move to Gillham, leaving Aaron behind. Aaron couldn't blame him, and he didn't most days. He missed his friend, though, and he wasn't surprised that his first instinct had been to come to find him.

"What did you do?" Adam asked as he sat in front of Aaron.

Aaron rubbed his face with his hands. "I fought with my dads."

"I want details. You wouldn't be here if it was just a normal fight."

"I don't know about that. It *was* a normal fight. I wanted to talk to them about what I'm supposed to do next, but they didn't have time for me, and when they finally had a few minutes, they forbid me to do what I wanted to do."

Adam leaned back in his chair and arched a brow. "Hunting vampires? Really, Aaron?"

Aaron bristled. "Who told you that?"

"Emery. He was worried you might have started already and that you were in danger."

"I'm surprised he cares."

Adam shook his head. He looked tired, which Aaron supposed made sense. He hadn't just met his mate and bonded with him. He'd moved to Gillham because Sterling's parents had died, and he and Adam needed to take care of his siblings. It couldn't be easy to become a father figure at his age and so quickly, even though one of Sterling's brothers was already a teenager.

"You're acting like a child," Adam said. "Which isn't surprising, since you're only nineteen, but still. Why are you giving your parents so much grief?"

"I didn't come here for you to berate me the way they did."

"Then you shouldn't have come, because they're right. Look, I know how you feel when it comes to your siblings. You're jealous. Anyone would be in your place."

"It's not that," Aaron protested, even though it was *exactly* that.

Adam seemed to know it from his expression. "You *are* jealous. You were an only child for fifteen years. Then suddenly, you had two siblings. It takes time to get used to, but it's been four years, Aaron. Your parents will always be your parents, but you have to give them space."

"I give them so much space they don't bother looking at me most days," Aaron snapped.

"And it's a problem. I won't deny that. I also won't deny that your siblings are only four and eight years old. You're nineteen. Instead of helping your parents with them, you're here pouting and complaining that your parents don't give you enough attention. Have you thought that maybe it's because they don't have the time? And what's that stupid idea of becoming a vampire hunter?"

"It's not stupid. You know what my father is. It's in our blood, and it's better than doing what I'm doing now, which is nothing."

"You could go to college. You could find a job somewhere. You have more opportunities than most people do, yet you want to hunt vampires?"

"Why not?"

"Why would you want to do it? You've never been interested in that. You like when your father tells you about it, but only because you like spending time with him. What changed? You don't even know where to start when it comes to hunting vampires, and you're not a fighter. Besides, even your dad stopped, and he did it for decades. Doesn't that tell you something?"

Aaron tightened his hands around his coffee cup and glared. "It tells me you're not supportive."

"I can't be when what you're talking about doing is stupid. You're going to get yourself killed, and where would that leave all of us? No matter how you feel about your fathers, they both love you, and they would be destroyed if something happened to you. They might not have gone about it the right way, but again, what did you expect? They're exhausted. They should be able to count on you, but instead, they have to deal with three unruly children."

This wasn't what Aaron had come here for, and he didn't want to listen to it anymore. He got to his feet, the chair slamming against the wall, making half the coffee shop turn to stare at them. Aaron didn't care. "I thought you were my friend," he spat out.

"I am. That's why I'm telling you the truth. You can't be a hunter. You're going to get yourself killed, which none of us want. Call your dads. Apologize to them and make peace with them. Your life isn't perfect, but trust me, it's better than a lot of people's lives. At least *you* still have your parents."

A flash of guilt threatened to change Aaron's mind, but he couldn't allow it. "It's as if I don't, so what's the difference?"

He turned around and left. Adam called out, but he didn't

stop. It seemed like these days, everyone he talked to told him to stop behaving like a child, but he didn't feel that was what he was doing.

Was he wrong?

James was exhausted, and he was glad he'd be able to go home soon. He just had to finish cleaning up and prepping stuff for tomorrow. He didn't feel like it, but prepping meant that he could come an hour later, which meant four AM instead of three. It gave him one hour more to sleep, and he would never say no to that.

He was surprised he'd managed to send Al to bed early. Usually, Al trudged on until they were done and everything was locked up. James was pleased he'd been trusted with the keys, even though he knew it was a spare set. He'd been working at the bakery for a while now, and his boss knew he was trustworthy. Still, this felt like a huge step forward, and James couldn't stop smiling, even though he was tired.

He wasn't surprised to see the sky was already dark when he opened the back door to take the trash out. It was late, and he was glad he'd remembered to text his mother to tell her he wasn't coming home just yet. She'd been worried, but he'd explained that he was just finishing up the work. She would never tell him to abandon everything to come home just because he was late for dinner.

Still, he couldn't wait to get to his bed, so he rushed toward the trash cans. He stopped when he noticed something against the wall, wondering what it was. The alley was illuminated, but only right above the back door. The trash cans should be closer, but it had never been a problem. Right now, though, James was wary.

It was probably nothing. It could be a raccoon, but it wasn't moving, and besides, they tended to stay away from businesses where shifters worked. James was a wolf shifter, and raccoons didn't like him. It could be sick, though, or worse, dead.

James did *not* need to deal with a dead raccoon tonight.

He moved closer until he could see that the thing against the wall wasn't an animal. It also wasn't dead, or at least, he hoped so, because he also wasn't up to dealing with a dead *person*.

Maybe the guy was homeless. James couldn't *not* think about how Lee had met his mate. He'd been working at the shelter, and just like James now, he'd been throwing out trash. His mate had been in the alley, and when Lee had realized they were mates, he'd had to work hard to convince Telyn he wasn't lying. Telyn was a demon, which meant he didn't have a mate. He didn't know how it felt to meet his, and with everything that happened to him with his mother, he didn't trust anyone.

All that was in the past now, though. Telyn lived with Lee, and he was safe and happy. They both were. James seriously doubted that the guy asleep against the wall was his mate, but he had to do something.

He moved even closer, startling when he realized the guy was Aaron. He couldn't help but wonder what he was doing there. Aaron lived in Whitedell, and unlike Telyn, he had a good family. His presence here didn't make sense.

He reached out with his foot and poked at Aaron's shoe. Aaron didn't react right away, so James poked even harder. That made Aaron jerk, and he scrambled to his feet, his back pressed against the wall.

"What do you want?" Aaron asked.

James opened the trashcan and threw the bag into it. Then, he crossed his arms over his chest and stared at Aaron. "What are you doing here?"

Aaron looked around, his gaze stopping on James again.

"What did it look like I was doing?"

"You were sleeping against the wall."

"How is that your business?"

"It's my business because I work here. I know you're not homeless. You should go home to your family."

James knew those words had been a mistake when he saw how Aaron reacted to them. His shoulders straightened, and he looked taller and bigger. He didn't shift to his harpy form, but James thought it was a close thing.

"What do you know about my family?" Aaron snapped.

"I know who you are. I'm a member of the Gillham pack. I know Adam, too. I don't know what's happening to you, but you should go home. You don't have a reason to sleep in a dark alley."

"You don't know anything about my life or my family," Aaron said, taking a step closer. "Stop talking about them."

James didn't want to fight. He didn't have the energy, and he was pretty sure Aaron could kick his ass if he shifted. He'd never seen him shifted from up close, but he knew Aaron became taller and more muscular. James was already exhausted as it was, and the thought of getting his ass kicked didn't appeal to him, even though Aaron was pretty.

Come to think of it, Aaron would probably kick his ass just because James had thought that.

James raised his hands. "I didn't mean to offend you. And you're right. I don't know anything about you or your family. It's obvious something's going on, though. I know you arrived in Gillham early this morning, and now, you're still here. Did you run away from home?"

Aaron snorted. "I'm nineteen."

"So? How does that stop you from running away?"

"I didn't run away from home. I just had a fight with my fathers."

James thought that sounded an awful lot like running

away from home, but he didn't point it out. "You should call them and make peace with them. You don't have to sleep here. It's going to be cold tonight, and this is far from comfortable. If you really don't want to go home, I can give you the address of a few bed and breakfasts."

"Or you can mind your own business. What do you care where I sleep tonight?"

James was trying to help Aaron, but the asshole didn't seem to care. Maybe it was time for James to stop being nice. "I don't. As far as I'm concerned, you can sleep in the middle of the street if you want to. But this is a place of business, and I can't have you loitering around like you might rob the place."

"I'm not loitering, and I'm not going to rob you," Aaron protested.

"Aren't you? Like you pointed out, I don't know you. How am I supposed to know that you're not waiting for the shop to be empty to break in? I should probably call the police, come to think of it."

"I didn't do anything!"

"Yet. But again, I don't know you. You could be planning on robbing the place."

James wasn't surprised when Aaron moved forward. He had to take a step back, and since the alley wasn't large, his back hit the wall.

He was scared. He couldn't deny that. Aaron was a harpy shifter, and it wouldn't take him much to hurt James. James hoped it wouldn't come to that, but what did he know?

Aaron got right up into James's face. "Who the fuck do you think I am? A thief? Why would I want to rob a bakery? I don't need cupcakes."

"Then go home," James tried again.

"Don't you think I would if I could?" Aaron snapped. He moved even closer, until their chests almost pressed together.

That was when James smelled it. In the beginning, he thought it was a mistake. Then he thought that someone must have passed on the main street, and that was who he was smelling. When Aaron moved again, though, he couldn't deny it.

He was the one who smelled like James's mate.

James's head spun. There was no way this could be happening. He'd just been complaining to Lee that he was an adult, yet he hadn't met his mate. He wasn't even sure he *wanted* to meet his mate.

He supposed he didn't have a choice because no matter how unbelievable it was, James couldn't deny that Aaron smelled like mate. He was pretty sure Aaron hadn't noticed. He was still trying to get James to fight him, but James wasn't about to give him satisfaction, not when it came to that. Instead, he straightened, hoping to show Aaron that he wouldn't be pushed into anything. "You should take a step back," he said slowly.

Aaron was angry. Part of him knew he shouldn't take it up with this guy, but he couldn't seem to stop himself. He didn't even know the guy's name, but the guy clearly knew him, which for some reason made Aaron even angrier.

"I'm not going to step back," he said.

The guy shook his head. "You really should. I don't want to fight with you, Aaron."

"Why not? Even though you know me, I have no idea who you are. What's it going to change if you fight with me?"

"My name is James. I'm a member of the Gillham pack. I've never talked to you, but I've seen you around, and I know you're Adam's friend. I also know Adam wouldn't be happy if he found out we fought in the bakery's back alley, and my boss wouldn't be, either. I don't want to get fired because of you."

"Go back inside, then."

James was still staring. His eyes were wide, but he seemed to be trying to get himself under control.

Aaron didn't understand why. He'd never been one to fight, but sometimes, it felt good to let go.

"Take a deep breath," James said.

Aaron's thoughts stuttered. "You want me to take a breath?"

"Please. You'll understand when you do."

Aaron didn't want James or anyone else to tell him what to do, but he couldn't stop himself. He took a deep breath, half smiling at the scent of sugar, yeast, melted butter, ginger, and a lot of other things that made him hungry. It smelled like a bakery, which made sense since they were standing next to one.

It didn't come from behind Aaron, though. The smell came from in front of him, and now, he understood why James' eyes were wide.

Aaron jerked back. "That's not possible."

"I don't know what it is or isn't, but we can't deny it. We're mates."

"We can't be."

James crossed his arms over his chest. "Well, I suppose I should have expected it—way to destroy a guy's ego, though. You could look a bit less disgusted by the knowledge that I'm your mate. I would be grateful."

Aaron shook his head and moved away even more. He wasn't disgusted by the thought of having a mate, but this was too much. "You can't be my mate," he repeated. He needed to put his thoughts in order, but how?

"You already said that. I'm sorry you have a mate you clearly don't want, but it's not like I wanted this, either. It happened, though, and we have to deal with it, whether we like it or not."

They didn't *have* to deal with it. Aaron could run away and never come back. He didn't have to see James ever again if he didn't want to. Right now, that sounded really fucking good, and he shifted without even thinking about it. He felt his wings spread from his back, and James sucked in a breath.

Aaron hadn't wanted to scare him, but he needed out. He'd come to Gillham to find a solution, to make decisions about his life, and now, he'd been thrown a curveball. He didn't even know what he wanted to do with his life. How was he supposed to deal with a mate, too?

He flapped his wings and took to the air. James was still standing there, staring, but Aaron's movements seemed to snap him into motion. "What do you think you're doing? We have to talk about this," he yelled.

There was nothing Aaron wanted less than to talk to James about them being mates, though, so he ignored him and flew away. Once again, he could hear James calling out for him, but he ignored it.

These days, he made it a habit to ignore people who called him and walk away from them.

Or fly away in this case.

He felt guilty, but he couldn't stop. He was overwhelmed and not ready to deal with the fact that James was his mate. He didn't want a mate.

Aaron was only nineteen. It was way too soon for him to settle down and have kids and all that stuff. He wasn't even sure he *wanted* kids. He hadn't started living, and having a mate would put a stop to all his plans, even though he didn't have any. No, the best thing he could do was to stay away from James. He was pretty sure that eventually, James would understand. From the looks of it, he had to be as young as Aaron. Surely he wouldn't want to settle down at nineteen and start having children and bond?

The thoughts ran around Aaron's mind, and he was unable to stop them. He needed a place to stay, but he couldn't go home. It was late, and he didn't want to face his dads, especially after what had just happened. They would see he was all over the place, and they would try to get answers out of him. In any other circumstance, he wouldn't have cared. He would have been happy because it would have meant they were interested in him and his life. Right now, though, he couldn't talk about this.

So instead of turning toward Whitedell, he headed to pack territory. It was a gamble, since James had said he was a member, and he might live there, but Aaron couldn't see another way. He couldn't find another place to spend the night, and he needed his best friend. Adam probably wouldn't be happy to see him, but he would put up with him.

Hopefully.

Aaron had no idea how long it was before he landed on Adam's porch. The lights were on inside, and he could hear noises, people talking, and smell food. It was dinner time, and now that he was here, he hesitated to interrupt.

Adam might be his best friend, but he had his own life. He hadn't freaked out when he'd met Sterling. Instead, he'd been there for his mate when Sterling's parents had died. He'd been his rock, and they'd settled down in a happy life together. They were bonded, and even though the children they were raising weren't theirs, they were effectively parents. Adam hadn't reacted the way Aaron just had when he'd realized who James was. He'd been more mature, like an adult, where Aaron had acted like a child. He'd flown away from his mate, for fuck's sake.

"Are you going to pout on my porch the entire night?" a voice asked.

Aaron jerked and almost stumbled down the porch steps. The only reason he didn't was his wings. He glared at

Sterling, who was standing in the open front door. How had Aaron not even heard him? "I'm not pouting," he said.

"Could have fooled me." Sterling's expression softened. "Adam didn't tell me what's going on, but I can see there's a problem. I won't ask you what it is because I know we're not exactly friends. I want you to know that you can stay here for however long you want, though."

"Why?" This was too much. Aaron needed time to wrap his mind around everything that was happening, but it felt like life was throwing one curveball after another at his face, and he couldn't avoid any of them.

"Because you're my mate's best friend. Because I know how it is to be vulnerable and to have your life tilt upside down when you least expect it."

"My parents didn't die."

Sterling smiled. "That's good. Trust me, I know parents can be annoying and all of that, but they're better alive than dead. You don't have to talk about whatever's going on with you. Just come and have dinner with us, all right? You can stay the night and talk to Adam tomorrow morning."

Aaron snorted. "Because he's going to let me wait until tomorrow morning."

"Maybe not, but you can go to bed as soon as you're done eating. He'll understand. Come on. Come sit with the family."

Sterling stepped aside, and Aaron quickly shifted before walking into the house. He was still as overwhelmed as he had been minutes earlier, but also more grounded. Whatever happened with his parents and James, he knew he wouldn't lose Adam.

He couldn't afford to.

James stared at the sky for what had to be minutes rather than seconds. He couldn't believe Aaron had just run away from him.

Would it be so bad to be James's mate? Aaron had seemed to think so. James wanted to give himself the benefit of the doubt, but he wasn't sure he could. Aaron had panicked when he'd realized they were mates. He'd flown away, and he hadn't looked back. That had to mean something, and it was hard for James to think it didn't have anything to do with him.

So James's mate didn't want him. He supposed that answered the question of whether or not he would ever meet his mate and share a life with them. The answer to that seemed to be no, and he needed to get moving.

He swallowed even though it hurt, and turned toward the bakery. He had to focus on what he *could* do right now, which was closing the bakery and heading home before his mother freaked out and called the police. Maybe it would help James not to obsess over Aaron's reaction to the knowledge they were mates.

He went through the next few minutes on autopilot. This wasn't the first time he closed the bakery, although usually, his boss was there. Al wasn't tonight, and while James would normally have been elated, now, he couldn't stop thinking about Aaron. He couldn't go home and face his parents right now. His mom would know something was wrong with him, and while she wouldn't push, he knew he would break down and tell her everything. She would try to help, but he didn't think he could take her kind words right now.

Once he was in his car, he texted her, telling her he would be having dinner with Lee and Telyn. He apologized, but she didn't seem to care. She was happy he was spending time with his brother, and of course, Telyn. She wanted the demon to feel at home with their family, but she was having a hard time convincing him he was part of it.

James texted Lee, too, before turning on the engine and driving toward his brother's apartment. He heard the phone vibrate on the seat next to his, but he didn't look until he was parked in front of Lee's building.

You're always welcome. We'll be waiting for you.

That was Lee's answer, and it made James's eyes prickle with tears. He didn't want to cry, though. It didn't make sense for him to feel like his heart was breaking. He'd never talked to Aaron before tonight. Why should he or his wolf care that their mate had rejected them? At the end of the day, Aaron was just a guy. He might be the perfect guy for them, but that didn't mean they couldn't be happy with someone else.

That thought didn't help James as much as he wished it did.

Just like Lee had said, he and Telyn were waiting for James. Both of them knew something had happened, and Telyn went to the kitchen after a few minutes, giving Lee and James time and space to talk.

"What's going on?" Lee asked quietly. "It's not our parents, is it? Or Kendall?"

James shook his head. "Everyone's fine. Don't worry about them. It's personal."

"Telyn won't be back until I call him. You can talk."

James almost started to, but he stopped. "We should talk over dinner. I'm sure he'll want to hear what's going on, too."

"He's worried about you, so I think he does, but he knows you're not comfortable with him."

James blinked. "Of course I'm comfortable with him. He's the one who's not comfortable with me or the rest of the family."

Lee smiled. "I told him that was what was happening, but he wanted to be sure you would be comfortable with him around, especially since you're obviously overwhelmed. As long as you're okay with it, we can talk while eating."

James wasn't hungry, but Lee and Telyn had opened their home to him. He wasn't going to offend them by telling them he didn't want to eat and that he only wanted them to listen to what he had to say.

Once they sat around the table, he pushed his food around his plate. Neither Lee nor Telyn asked him what was going on, and James was both relieved and annoyed. He wanted someone to get the story out of him. He didn't want to have to think about how to tell them—showing them how much he had to be ashamed of.

"Do you guys know Aaron?" he eventually asked.

Telyn shook his head, but Lee nodded. "He's Adam's friend, isn't he?" He looked at his mate. "The harpy."

"I see. I don't know him, but I know *of* him," Telyn said quietly.

"The same goes for me," James told him. "I'm not friends with Adam or even Sterling. Sterling's a few years older than me, and while Adam is twenty, he didn't grow up here. I suppose you can say we're friendly, but not close. I do know that Aaron is Adam's friend, though."

"What's going on with him, then?" Lee asked.

"He's in town. I don't know what's wrong, but it's obvious something is. He arrived early this morning. I saw him when I got to the bakery. And tonight, when I took out the trash, he was sleeping in the alley."

Lee frowned. "Sleeping in the alley?"

"I don't think he's homeless. He's a Whitedell pride member, and they would never kick anyone out, not unless they did something truly horrible. It does look like he ran away from home, though."

"Isn't he a bit old to run away from home?"

"He told me he's nineteen. I don't know what happened to him, but I do know that when he found out I was his mate, he flew away."

There was a moment of silence, and James looked down at his plate. He could feel Telyn and Lee staring at him, and he didn't think he had the strength to stare back.

"He flew away?" Lee eventually asked.

James nodded curtly. "I suppose that answers the question as to what he thinks of me."

"I don't think it does," Telyn said. "When I first met Lee, I was terrified, and I pushed him away."

"That's because you didn't believe you were mates. You couldn't feel it."

Telyn nodded. "I still can't. I trust him now, though. The fact that Aaron *can* tell you're his mate doesn't mean he's not afraid. You said yourself that something is obviously going on with him. The fact that he left might not have anything to do with you. You don't know much about him. You should probably try talking to him before assuming he doesn't want you."

Telyn was right. It was hard to admit, though. "What if he truly doesn't want me? He didn't look scared when he realized. He looked horrified, as if he couldn't think of anything worse than being my mate."

"But you don't know anything about him," Telyn repeated. "It could be that he doesn't want you, but why should he react that way? He doesn't know you. I think that there's probably something big going on in his life right now, and finding his mate was overwhelming. There's also the fact that he's young, and so are you. Maybe he thinks you'll demand too much from him. You said he's Adam's friend, and Adam's only twenty. He and Sterling already bonded. Maybe Aaron thinks you'll want the same."

James couldn't think of anything worse. He might have met his mate, but he was nowhere near ready to bond with him, and it didn't have anything to do with the fact that they hadn't even talked about it. "I'm twenty. I'm not going to ask him to bond and settle down with me right now. We're way too young." And from the looks of it, Aaron was also immature.

"Exactly," Telyn agreed. "It might have been an impulse to run away. Don't dismiss it, but don't obsess over it, either. You won't know what's going on until you talk to him. That's what you should do tomorrow, as soon as you can."

"I can't go to Whitedell, though. I have work."

"Then do the next best thing," Lee intervened. "You might not be able to talk to Aaron, but Adam is right here. He should be able to give you an insight into his best friend."

It felt a bit like a betrayal, but James wasn't sure he could face Aaron after Aaron's reaction to them being mates. Adam did seem like the next best thing, and this way, James would be prepared when he next faced Aaron.

If he ever did.

Chapter Three

The house was silent, which was strange. Every time Aaron was here, it was noisy with screaming and the sound of kids running. One of Sterling's siblings was sixteen, but the other two were six-year-old twins, and they were never silent. Spending time at Adam's house felt like being at home, which was one of the reasons Aaron didn't usually spend the night. If he wanted noise and children, he could stay in Whitedell.

He extracted himself from the bed in the guest room and opened the door. He tried to remember why it would be so silent, but he couldn't come up with anything, at least until he walked into the kitchen downstairs and saw that both Sterling and Adam were sitting at the table. They were alone, and Aaron remembered that it was the middle of the week, which meant the children would be in school.

"Good morning," Sterling said. He smiled at Aaron, and Aaron smiled back.

Maybe he should spend more time here. He liked Sterling, and he didn't know him well enough. He also missed his best friend. "Good morning."

"Do you want coffee?"

"Please."

Sterling got to his feet and moved toward the coffee machine. Adam, on the other hand, patted the chair next to him. "Park your ass here and tell me what happened. I've been dying since last night, but Sterling convinced me not to push. Is it still your parents? Because I didn't mean to be so harsh. I'm sorry if I offended you."

Aaron sat, shaking his head. "I won't deny that you were harsh, but I think I needed it. I probably still do."

"So you're headed home today?"

Aaron hesitated. He should go back to Whitedell, but now, there was a complication. "I don't know. I think I need some time away from everything. I love my dads. You know I do, and I love my siblings, too. And you *are* right that I was jealous. I'm still trying to work through that, even though it's been four years. I don't think I would mind if my parents had time for me, but they're focused on my sister and brother, and I feel abandoned. If they could just give me a little more time, I would be happier."

"I don't think you realize how hard it is to have young children," Sterling said as he sat back at the table. He placed a coffee mug in front of Aaron, and Aaron wrapped his fingers around it after smiling at him.

"I do understand. I was already fifteen when we adopted my sister and my brother was born. I saw how much work it was."

"Yet you don't help them," Adam pointed out.

Aaron scowled. "I thought you were sorry for being so harsh."

"I shouldn't have said what I said the way I said it, but it doesn't change the fact that I still think I was right. You're nineteen, Aaron. Yes, it's hard not to be the center of your parents' life anymore, but you're old enough to understand and deal with it. If you truly want your parents to spend more time with you, take care of your siblings so they don't have to do it all the time. I'm sure they want to spend more time with you and together, just the two of them. Instead, they have work, they have your brother and your sister, and you moping your way around."

Aaron was tempted to leave, but he stayed right where he was. He knew he was lucky. He only had to look at Sterling to understand that. Sterling and his siblings had lost their parents. Aaron's might not devote as much time to him as before, but they were still alive, and eventually, his siblings would grow up. Sterling would never have the opportunity to see his parents again, but Aaron did. He had to stop whining and help more.

That didn't solve any of his other problems, though.

"Your parents love you," Sterling murmured. "They're busy. I remember when the twins were born. It was hard. I was sixteen, while Kendall was ten. We had to wrap our minds around the fact that they weren't just our parents anymore and learn how to be a bigger family. That's not going to happen if you keep running away. Adam is right. You're going to lose them if you continue, and I don't think you want that. I'm sure *they* don't."

Aaron sighed. "Fine. You're right."

Adam sucked in a breath. "Did you hear that, Sterling? He said we were right. Are we sure this is really Aaron? He could be a pod person."

Aaron scowled and tried to kick him under the table. Adam laughed and moved away, and the tension that had been weighing over the kitchen let up. "I'll talk to them later today," Aaron said.

"Will you be going back to Whitedell?" Adam asked.

"I don't know. There's something else, something that happened yesterday."

"What? Is it the reason you came here instead of going home last night?"

"No. I was going to stay in Gillham regardless. I was sleeping in an alley in town. I was angry at my fathers, and I guess I wanted to punish them. I know it was wrong now," he quickly added before Adam could yell at him.

Adam shook his head. "Sometimes, I can't believe you. You were going to sleep on the street so that you could get even with your parents?"

"Not even, no. But even though I know I was wrong, I still have no idea what to do with my life, and meeting my mate hasn't helped."

Adam gaped. "You met your mate?"

Aaron tapped his fingertips on the side of his mug. It was still warm. "Last night, yes. He's a Gillham pack member. His name is James."

Sterling's expression turned thoughtful. "Well, James is a common name. I can think of at least a few in the pack."

"He works at the bakery. He's about my age."

Sterling nodded. "I think I know him. We're not friends, but yes. We're about the same age. So he's your mate?"

"He is. And I probably ruined everything." Aaron didn't know if he wanted to be with James, but he was pretty sure that flying away and leaving his mate behind was *not* the way to do things.

"What did you do? Fly away?" Adam asked, humor in his tone. Aaron stared at him until Adam's eyes widened. "You flew away from him? I can't believe it." He paused and cocked his head. "Actually, I think I can. *Of course* you'd fly away from him."

Aaron raked a hand through his hair. "It's overwhelming. I was already fighting with my parents, and I was terrified. I'm not ready to bond and have kids and settle down."

Adam's eyebrows shot high on his forehead. "That's what James wants?"

"I don't know. I didn't give him time to talk."

"So you ran away even though you have no idea what he wants. Did I get that right?"

Aaron was tempted to throw something at his friend's head, but unfortunately, he needed the coffee in his mug. "I panicked. I was overwhelmed by the fight with my parents and not knowing what I want to do with my life."

"As long as you don't get yourself killed hunting vampires, I don't think anyone cares. Do whatever you want."

"I don't *know* what I want."

Adam's expression softened. "You're only nineteen, and you're a shifter. You can live to be a hundred and fifty. No one expects you to know what you want to do right now, and even if you do, you could change your mind dozens of times, and no one would care. You have time to change your mind and a great support system. Did your parents push you to make a decision? Is that why you feel like you have to do something?"

Aaron shook his head. "No. They would never do something like that. They told me I could go to college or take my time finding a job I like."

"Is what you want to do really vampire hunting?"

"I don't know."

Adam reached out and patted Aaron's hand. "Don't make rash decisions, and please, talk to your parents and your mate. I think that before finding a job, you have to fix your life and your relationships. You can't know what James wants if you don't talk to him, and you were cruel flying away from him."

Aaron sighed. "I have some groveling to do, don't I?"

Adam grinned. "A lot of it, and I wish I could be there to watch."

James sucked in a breath. He stared at the house in front of him, wondering if he was doing the right thing.

He needed to talk to Aaron, but he had no idea how to find him. The easiest way would be to go to Whitedell, but could he really do that? He didn't want to invade Aaron's home. It was clear Aaron didn't want to see him, and James didn't want to push. He'd had time to think about it and wrap his mind around what had happened, and he understood better why Aaron had run away.

He was tempted to do the same just now.

Finding your mate at twenty was overwhelming. James hadn't thought much about it when Lee had met Telyn, but he should have. Maybe it was different. Lee had been more than happy to meet Telyn, and James hoped that eventually, he would be, too. He only had one mate, and he didn't want to lose him before they even had a chance. He hoped that if he talked to Aaron, they could fix whatever was broken.

That wouldn't happen if he didn't get at least an inkling of what Aaron was thinking, though. He didn't think Adam would betray his friend, but maybe he could give James a few pointers. He was going to need them.

Before he could change his mind, he climbed the porch steps and knocked on the door. The house was silent, which made sense, since it was a school day. Sterling often came into the bakery with his younger siblings, although since James worked in the back, he didn't have the opportunity to talk to him. Maybe he should make more of an effort, especially now that he'd found out that he and Aaron were mates. That didn't mean Aaron would want to be with him, though, so maybe becoming friends with Adam's best friend's mate was overstepping.

Why did all of this have to be so complicated?

The door opened, and Adam stood there. He blinked at James. "Yes?"

James held up the box of cupcakes he'd brought. He'd had to ask his boss for a few hours off work today, but he'd made sure to come in early so Al wouldn't have a reason to say no. He hadn't even asked why James wanted the time off. "My name is James. I brought cupcakes."

Adam looked at the box. "I can see that." His eyes narrowed. "Wait. I know you. You work at the bakery?"

James nodded. "I do, which is why I brought cupcakes. I know they're not breakfast food, but they're delicious."

Adam snatched the box from James's fingers. "Everything is breakfast food. You're here for Aaron, aren't you?"

James blinked. "I am. Did he tell you about me?"

"He did. He came here last night. He's still here."

James sucked in a breath. "Maybe I should go."

"Don't you want to talk to him?"

"I do, but I don't want him to be uncomfortable, and I'm pretty sure that's what would happen if I tried talking to him. He didn't take it well the last time I did."

Adam snorted. "That's an understatement, from what I know of the situation. You don't have to stay if you don't want to, but if you want to talk to him, he's here. Maybe you should give him at least the opportunity to say yes or no to that."

James felt numb, which he supposed was better than being terrified. It would be too easy for Aaron to reject him again, and he wasn't sure he could go through that a second time, especially not if it was so spectacular. Even though Aaron had run away from him, he'd looked gorgeous. It was the first time James had seen him from up close, and he truly looked more like an angel than a harpy.

"Why don't you come in?" Adam said gently. "You two don't *have* to talk. He'll be surprised to see you, but I think he'll be pleased, too."

"I wouldn't be too sure about that."

Adam grimaced. "I know he didn't behave well last night, and I won't apologize for him, but I do want to tell you there were extenuating circumstances. He was overwhelmed, both because of the fact that you two are mates and because of what's happening in the rest of his life. Give him a chance to explain, yeah?"

James could only nod. He was wary, but he knew he and

Aaron had to do this. They had to talk, if anything, to decide whether or not they should see each other again.

He followed Adam inside the house. He could hear voices, and he wasn't surprised when Adam led him to the kitchen. Aaron and Sterling were sitting at the table. They both looked up when they heard them come in. Adam raised the box he was still holding. "James brought cupcakes."

Sterling smiled, but Aaron kept staring at James until James wanted to leave. Instead of doing that, he stared back.

They were both hesitant. James didn't want to take the first step, but he thought he would have to if he wanted this to happen. "Good morning," he said, still looking at Aaron. "I think we should talk."

Aaron nodded. "I think we should, yes."

"We're going to take these cupcakes upstairs," Adam said.

Aaron frowned. "You don't have to go."

"We do. We always take advantage of the fact that the kids are in school to be together." Adam wiggled his eyebrows.

Sterling made a strangled sound, while Aaron blushed and glared at his friend. "You did *not* have to say that."

"I just wanted the two of you to know we'd be busy. Take all the time you need." He paused and looked from one to the other. "Talk things out, but don't fight. I'll kick both your asses if you do."

James was amused, and he pressed his lips together as Sterling and Adam left the kitchen. Why hadn't he ever tried to become friends with them? They seemed like good people, and they could have used his help when Sterling's parents had died, although actually they'd had plenty of help. He supposed they'd be at least friendly from now on if Aaron wanted to see where things could go between him and James. It all depended on him, and James had no idea how this would go.

James shuffled his feet, unsure where to start. He'd had

time to think, but he wasn't sure Aaron had. "So," he said.

"So," Aaron repeated when James didn't continue. He rubbed the back of his neck. "I should apologize. I shouldn't have left the way I did last night."

"It was quite dramatic." And James wouldn't mind seeing Aaron's wings again, but under other circumstances.

Aaron smiled sarcastically. "That's me. If you ask my parents, they'll tell you I'm the king of drama. They wouldn't be wrong, either." He sucked in a breath. "But I *am* sorry. I shouldn't have flown away, not without talking to you. I panicked."

James gestured at the chairs around the kitchen table. "Can I sit down?"

"Of course. You should get comfortable."

James was pretty sure nothing in this situation could be comfortable, but he sat in front of Aaron. He linked his fingers on top of the table before unlinking them and pressing his palms to his thighs. He swallowed. Why was this so hard?

"I should tell you why I ran," Aaron said.

"Only if you want to. I don't want to push you to do or say anything you're not ready for."

Aaron shrugged. "We're going to have to talk about this sooner or later, and I guess now is as good a moment as any. Besides, we have to make a decision. We can't stay in this situation without moving forward or backward. It wouldn't be fair for you to make decisions without knowing everything there is to know."

James steeled himself. He was pretty sure he wasn't going to like whatever Aaron was about to tell him.

Aaron had to choose his words carefully. "I was being a brat," he ended up saying.

James snorted and tried to make it sound like a cough. "I

wouldn't say that."

"You should, though. It's not just with you. It was also with my parents, and I'm going to call them and apologize as soon as we're done here." Aaron swallowed. "I'm nineteen. I was an only child until I was fifteen. Then my parents adopted my sister, Hazel, and my father got pregnant with my brother, Matthew."

James blinked. "Did you say that your *father* got pregnant?"

Sometimes, Aaron forgot that people outside the pride didn't know about his father. It wasn't a secret, but it also wasn't something he talked about to people. "It's complicated. You should probably know, though. My father was human until he was kidnapped and taken to one of those labs."

James nodded. "I know about them. Several of my pack members spent time there, too."

"Well, my father came out not quite human anymore. He was half harpy, which was hard for him to get used to. He'd never been a shifter, and it was done to him with pain and torture. The fact that harpies are only females also didn't make things easy on him. The change made it possible for him to get pregnant, and he didn't know about that until he actually did. It's not a normal pregnancy, either. He lays eggs."

James rubbed his face. "This is a lot to wrap my mind around."

"I know. I'm just telling you so you understand. All my life, I've never been normal. It's not just that one of my fathers is both human and harpy and that he carried me, and I was born from an egg. My other father is a Krsnik. It's a kind of shifter and vampire hybrid. So you see, I'm torn between four species, and unlike my fathers, I can shift both into a harpy form and into a white harpy eagle. It's always been hard for me, and it was even harder after my siblings came into my life. I didn't have my parents' attention anymore, and I acted like a brat. I still do."

"I can't say I understand. I'm a wolf shifter, and it's never been strange. I've never had to go through what you've had to go through."

"All in all, I didn't have to go through anything. My life was easy. I have two parents who love me and an extended family who would kill for me. I'm an oddity, though, and it makes it hard for me to relate to other people. It also makes it hard to choose how to live my life. I'm nineteen, which means I need to start thinking about going to college or getting a job, and I have no idea what to do." Aaron hesitated. "That's where you come in, at least in part."

"What do you mean?"

"I guess that after seeing Adam and Sterling together, I thought that you were going to want the same thing. I have plans, and having a mate would make me stuck."

James arched a brow. "You just said you don't have plans. You don't know what to do with your life."

"I'm not sure what to do, but I was thinking about hunting vampires like my father did before he met my dad. That's what Krsniks do. My father lost his entire family because of it. It's the family business, though." That wasn't entirely true, but so far, it was the only thing Aaron could think of doing.

"Why do you think I was going to try to stop you from doing that?" James asked.

"You're my mate," Aaron said, puzzled.

"And? You don't know me. I'm as young as you are, and I have no plans on settling down anytime soon, not even with you. That doesn't mean we never have to see each other again, but it also doesn't mean I can't have a life without you. I won't break down if you're not in my life."

"But I'm your mate. You only have one."

"So? The same goes for you, yet you don't seem to have a problem throwing me away."

"I'm not throwing you away," Aaron protested.

"You're not? Because to me, it sounds like that's what you're planning on doing. You were going to do it without even talking to me." James sucked in a breath. "Look, I understand you don't want to settle down and bond. I don't, either. It's way too soon. I'm only twenty, and I just started my apprenticeship at the bakery. I plan on making that a job, which means I have to stay in Gillham. I wouldn't want to leave anyway, not with my family here. You, on the other hand, are keen on not staying. Not only are you from Whitedell, but you just said you wanted to hunt vampires, and I doubt you'll find a lot of them here. That means we're going to have to choose. I don't want to go, and you don't want to stay. The choice is easy, isn't it?"

Aaron was dumbfounded. James had nailed the problem, and he seemed to be taking it incredibly well. Wasn't he at least a bit sad or angry at the thought of losing Aaron? "So that's it?"

"I don't see why we should make this complicated when it really isn't. You're going to go, and I'm going to stay. That means we both should find someone more suited to our lives. I won't care if you find a boyfriend or girlfriend. I won't hold it against you. The bond between us doesn't have to mean anything. We didn't choose it, and we shouldn't be tethered by it. Go on with your life as if you never met me, Aaron. I'll do the same."

"What are you talking about?"

"Our lives can't mesh, not if I want to have a bakery and you want to hunt vampires. But we're both young, and we'll be able to find someone else. You can continue hunting vampires with your significant other while I open a bakery and have a family. It's the best we can do, and I don't think we should stop ourselves from doing it just because some people think we have to be together because of the bond."

Aaron tightened his hands around his mug. It was getting cold now, like his heart. "You would give me up that easily? Doesn't the bond mean anything to you?"

"Of course the bond means something. It doesn't have to be the end-all, though. You don't want anything to do with me, and I'll get over it."

"How can you get over it? It's a mate bond. Even though we're not bonded, you have to feel it." Aaron certainly did. Right now, he wanted to drag James to his side of the table and kiss him until he stopped saying those things.

The only reason he didn't was that James was right, at least in part. If James wasn't willing to give up his life in Gillham and Aaron continued in his wish to hunt vampires and travel around the country, they couldn't work. They couldn't be together that way, but could he give up the mate bond that easily?

Aaron didn't know what he wanted, but he knew it wasn't this. He couldn't give up James, but he also couldn't be with him. What was he supposed to do now? How could he make this kind of vital decision at nineteen, when he was barely out of his teenage years? How had Adam? He hadn't hesitated to be there for Sterling when Sterling had needed him, and now, he had a family, a home, and he was a father figure. The thought of doing the same was terrifying, yet at the same time, Aaron couldn't let go of it.

He also couldn't let go of the fact that James didn't seem to have a problem with forgetting him and going on with his life.

Aaron was offended. It was plain to see, and it made James want to smile. He didn't, because he didn't want to offend Aaron even more, not when they were finally talking. "I do feel the bond between us," he confirmed.

"Then how can you give it up so easily?"

"It wouldn't be easy. What do you expect me to do, though? I don't want to give up what we have, but you clearly don't want it, and in the end, not everyone ends up with their mate. I can't force you into having a relationship with me or even talking to me. I don't want to get hung up on you when you'll end up leaving." Or worse since he was planning on becoming a vampire hunter. Were vampires even still around? James had no idea, and right now, he couldn't care less. He didn't want Aaron to leave or to get killed, but what could he do?

He and Aaron were mates, but that didn't mean anything. Just like he'd told Aaron, they could easily separate and find someone else to spend her life with. It might not be as easy as James hoped it would be, but still. He had no intention of yearning for Aaron, not when he was only twenty and still had at least a hundred years to live.

"You make it sound like you don't care."

James sighed. "I care." And very much so. He wanted what Lee and Telyn had. He wanted Aaron and him to get to know each other, to be together eventually. He had no intention of bonding or having children anytime soon, but maybe one day? It didn't seem like he would be with Aaron, though, not if Aaron insisted on becoming a vampire hunter.

"Why are you pushing me away, then?"

It was getting frustrating. "I'm not pushing you away. You're the one doing that. You want to live your own life without me, and that's okay. I'm not going to beg."

"I never expected you to."

"I don't understand what you want from me. When we met, you ran away. Now that we're talking, you made sure I knew that you have plans and that I wasn't part of them. You said you were planning on leaving, and I told you I couldn't. I think it makes it clear what we have to do, but now, you don't seem to want that, either. What *do* you want, then? For us to have a long-distance relationship? You want to hunt vampires while I stay at home? Do you really think we can do that?"

Aaron shook his head. "It wouldn't be fair to either of us. I also don't want to give up what we might have, though. I might have reacted harshly, but I know that meeting your mate is a once in a lifetime opportunity. We have an opportunity not many people have, and I don't want to give it up."

"I don't see another way, though." It broke James's heart, but he truly didn't. To make things work between them, one of them would have to give something up, and he didn't know if either of them were ready to do that.

"We can find a way," Aaron said. He sounded convinced.

"Maybe. We don't have to figure everything out today. Why don't you give me your phone number? That way, I can reach you, and I'll give you mine, too. We can talk and text and see what happens. We shouldn't make any promises, because I'm not sure either of us can keep them, but this, we can do." Even though it would be hard. James's instinct was to push Aaron away, since he so clearly didn't want anything to do with him. He was also confused, though. They both were.

Aaron was nineteen, while James was twenty. They were figuring out their lives, and it wasn't easy. Maybe figuring things out together would make it easier, but James didn't think so. They had to make their own decisions, and they couldn't think of the other while they did so.

He didn't want to lose Aaron, but he also couldn't leave Gillham. He couldn't leave his family or his job. He couldn't say he'd always wanted to be a baker, but now that he was doing it, he enjoyed it. He might change his mind in the future, but he knew he would never be a vampire hunter. He just couldn't do that kind of thing.

He didn't want Aaron to do it, either, but he didn't say that. It was Aaron's decision. James had no say in it, even though

Aaron wanted to do a dangerous job that would probably get him killed. He was pretty sure Aaron's parents and Adam would have enough to say about it anyway.

He checked his watch. "I should get back to work."

Aaron's eyes widened. "You're leaving?"

His tone made James want to stay, but he couldn't. "As you know, I work at the bakery. I took a few hours off to come here, but my boss expects me to come back soon. Besides, I don't think there's anything else we can say to each other. We know where we stand and that we have to make a decision."

"It's a decision that could change our entire lives."

"I know, which is why we should take time to think about it. Just know that I don't expect anything from you, Aaron. I don't want to lose the bond we could have, but I can't force you to stay, and I would never try. I also don't want you to come to resent me if you decide to give up your dreams of being a hunter to be with me. Think about it. Take your time. Text and call me and get to know me. Maybe once you do, it will be easier for you to make your decision." James doubted anything would change Aaron's mind, but still. He could hope.

Aaron was important to him because they were mates. If they hadn't been, he wouldn't have cared about what Aaron wanted to do with his life. They wouldn't have talked to begin with. But Aaron was his mate, and there was no changing that. If they gave up the chance to be together, they would never find this kind of relationship again.

James got to his feet. "I have to go."

"I don't want you to," Aaron confessed.

"It's the bond. We have to take time to think about this, though." James hesitated. "I know I made it sound like it would be all or nothing, but it doesn't have to be. If you want to go off hunting for a decade or two, then come back, you can. I can't promise I'll wait for you, though. I wouldn't expect you to wait for me or to be celibate. It's a risk you might have to take."

Aaron nodded. He looked sad, and James wanted to stay and comfort him, but he couldn't. He'd said what he had to say. He'd explained to Aaron what he did and didn't expect.

Now they both would have to make decisions.

Aaron was the one who held a lot in his hands. His decision could make or break their relationship, and James didn't like not having a say in it. The only thing he *could* do was tell Aaron that if he wanted to stay and try, he would be more than happy to go along with it. If Aaron decided to leave, though, James wouldn't try to stop him.

When he left the house, he heard Sterling and Adam upstairs. It made his cheeks heat, but it also made him wonder. They were mates, and they were obviously happy, even with all the sadness and pain Sterling had to deal with. Could James and Aaron have that? Could he have it with anyone else?

Because Aaron was his mate, and his wolf yearned to go back to the kitchen and drag him into their arms. James couldn't do that, and his wolf didn't understand why. For the wolf, things were easy. James and Aaron were mates, which meant they should be together.

They were also human, though. Their human side was what made everything much harder than it should be, and this time wasn't any different. James had no idea what would happen, and he was pretty sure Aaron didn't, either. Whether or not they managed to find their way to each other, they would have to compromise.

James wasn't sure Aaron could.

CHAPTER FOUR

Things were tense, and they'd been that way since Aaron had come home. His fathers were disappointed with him, but they didn't seem to want to talk about it, which in the beginning had been perfectly fine with Aaron. Now, though, he was starting to hate the situation.

He knew it was his fault. He shouldn't have run away from his parents, and he shouldn't have been stupid and stayed away. They loved him, and they wanted him to be safe. His jealousy pointed to the fact that he was a brat and an asshole, and that needed to change. He was trying to do just that, but everything else was still in the air.

What was he supposed to do now that he was an adult? His parents didn't want him to be a hunter, and he understood why. If he was honest with himself, he didn't think he could be that kind of person. From what his dad had told him, it was a lonely, dangerous life. Was it really what Aaron wanted to do for the next few decades? Did he want to stay away from his family and his mate to keep them safe?

Aaron had no answers, and he wished there was someone he could talk to. He could call Adam, he supposed, but Adam had been clear about what he thought of the situation. He'd made Aaron think, but Aaron doubted there was much more he could do to help.

So he'd been taking care of his siblings more than before. He hadn't talked to his parents about it, but he hoped they were pleased. He should have been doing this all along, and he realized how selfish he'd been. He didn't know how to apologize to them. The easiest way would be to tell them he was sorry, but he didn't feel strong enough.

Things couldn't stay the way they were, though. Aaron didn't want them to, and he also wondered if he and James could have a future.

They'd been texting, and they'd called each other a few times. Things were awkward between them. They didn't know each other, and they hadn't started their relationship in the best way. That was all Aaron's fault, too, but he truly wanted to fix things. He wasn't sure he could, and the situation with James, along with the one with his parents, made him feel unsteady. It was even worse than before, which was what he'd been trying to avoid.

The apartment was silent when he poked his head out of his room. That was strange, since his siblings were never silent, and he wondered what had happened. He left his bedroom and looked into his brother's room, then his sister's, but they weren't there. He was starting to panic, although he knew it was stupid. They were probably out with his dads, maybe playing with the other children somewhere in the mansion. Still, it was getting late, and his fathers insisted on the children having a daily routine. It was strange not to see anyone.

When Aaron stepped into the living room, his heart racing, he froze. His fathers were both on the couch, waiting for him. There was no sign of Matthew and Hazel.

"Nysys is babysitting," Emery said.

Aaron was relieved yet worried. "Is that a good idea? He's not exactly the best babysitter in the world."

"He's a good person. He'll make sure they don't get hurt. Besides, it won't be for long. Why don't you sit down?"

Aaron gingerly obeyed. It looked like it was time for them to talk. He'd expected it to happen ever since he'd come back, and he'd been surprised it hadn't yet. He should have known his fathers would want to take their time, which couldn't happen with his siblings around.

Emery was looking straight at Aaron, but Troy was avoiding his gaze. It broke Aaron's heart a little. It was his fault. He was the one who'd done that, and he wanted to fix it.

Emery cleared his throat. "We've already talked about my past as a hunter. I wanted to talk about it again, though. I'm not sure why you decided that's what you want to do with your life, and I'd like to find out. You know I lost everyone because of the hunting. I had a family. I had parents, siblings, aunts, and uncles. All of them are gone, killed by vampires. I was lucky to realize it was time to stop and to find this place. It meant I had a home, and I could leave hunting behind."

"I know all of that," Aaron said quietly.

"Then you understand why we don't want you to be a hunter. Why do you want to?"

Aaron looked down at his hands. "I'm not sure. I just feel like I have to do *something*. I'm nineteen, yet I'm here the entire day, doing nothing. I know I should have helped more with Hazel and Matthew, and I will from now on. But that doesn't help me understand what I should do now that I'm an adult."

"You don't *have* to do anything. I know that you usually should go to college or find a job once you finish high school. We're different, though. We're shifters, so you have more time. Your father and I don't want you to make decisions about the rest of your life right now. If what you want is time, then we're more than happy to make that happen."

"We can't forbid you to become a hunter," Troy continued. He still wasn't looking at Aaron. "Like you said, you're nineteen, and even though we're shifters, it means you're an adult. We'll support you if that's what you want to do, even though we don't agree with it."

Aaron was stunned. He'd expected his dads to forbid him

to do it, but instead, they were saying yes.

"We had another idea, though," Emery intervened. "As you know, when I first arrived in Whitedell, I was an enforcer. I'd left the vampire hunting behind. Is that something you might want to do?"

Aaron leaned back in the armchair he was sitting in. He wasn't sure why his mind had gone straight to hunting, but now, he regretted it. "I don't know."

"You would still be able to protect people and help them, but you would have a team. You would have people at your back, which is all we ask for. Being an enforcer is still dangerous, but it could be a compromise."

"What about what I am, though? Would they take me even though I'm a harpy and I can get pregnant?" Aaron had always been a freak of nature. He knew his bubble here in Whitedell was safe. No one would ever make fun of him for what he was, and it was easier and safest for him to stay at the mansion.

He would have been alone if he was a vampire hunter, but being an enforcer meant being with people. It meant having their backs and trusting them to have his. Could he really do that? Would they accept him, knowing what he was?

"What you are doesn't mean you can't be an enforcer," Troy said, his voice slightly harsh. "We can talk to the head of the enforcers, if it makes you feel better. He's the one who makes these decisions, and I'm sure he can find you the perfect team. That is, if you want to do this."

Aaron slowly nodded. "I'm not sure I do, but I think it would be best if we did talk to someone. I don't know why I wanted to be a hunter. I think it's more because I wanted to do something and to make the two of you proud than because I truly wanted to kill vampires."

"But don't you see?" Troy asked. His voice broke, and he had to swallow before going on. "We already are proud of you."

"I haven't done anything to make you proud."

"You don't have to. You're our son. I know the last few years especially haven't been easy on you. We never planned to have three children, but we couldn't give up Hazel once we adopted her. We should have talked to you more about it, and we should have devoted more time to you. It wasn't fair to focus so completely on Hazel and Matthew."

"It wasn't fair for me to be a brat about it. I know you don't have time, and that's fine. They need you more than I do."

Troy shook his head. "That's not true. You're still our son, even though you're nineteen. If there's anything wrong, if you need to talk, I want you to come to us. We'll make time for you from now on, I promise."

Aaron's throat felt tight, so he nodded. He couldn't say anything. He wasn't sure he needed to.

His fathers had listened to him. They knew what his problem was, and they were willing to try to fix it. He might become an enforcer, and he definitely wouldn't be a vampire hunter. He still had no idea what would happen with James, but still.

How had one conversation managed to fix most of his problems?

James wasn't sure if he should tell his parents about Aaron. He wanted to. He would have, in any other circumstance. But Aaron didn't know whether or not he wanted to be with James, and James didn't want to make his parents happy, then take that happiness away from them. If he told them he'd met his mate, they would be over the moon. They would expect him to have the same happiness they had together.

He wasn't sure that would ever happen.

He and Aaron had texted a few times. Things between

them were awkward, and he still wasn't sure Aaron would ever want him. He had big plans about becoming a vampire hunter, and James wasn't part of those plans. It shouldn't hurt as much as it did, but James couldn't deny it.

Even though he'd tried his best to show Aaron he wouldn't care, he did, and way too much.

He didn't know Aaron. That didn't change the fact that they were mates and that James knew that even though he could have other relationships, none of the guys he would be with would make him forget Aaron. It was impossible. The bond between them would always be there, even if they never did anything about it, and it made James angry.

Why did his mate have to be someone who didn't want him?

He was still clinging to the hope that maybe Aaron would change his mind. They'd agreed they were too young to make any kind of decision when it came to bonding and having a life together. James hadn't changed his mind about that, but he couldn't stop thinking about possibly having lost his mate. Even if they didn't bond right now, surely they could be together? They could get to know each other, maybe have a relationship. They wouldn't be the only ones in town to do that.

Aaron had to want it, too, though.

James jerked out of his thoughts when his phone rang. He looked down at his hands, dirty with flour and butter. He was so used to making cookies and whatnot that he barely had to think about the process as he did so, which was the only reason he hadn't ruined several batches by thinking about Aaron.

His phone had stopped ringing by the time he managed to clean his hands, and when he took it out of his pocket, he noticed he had a missed call and a text from Aaron. He looked around, knowing that Al wouldn't be happy if he saw James on his phone. Still, James wanted to know what Aaron had to say. Since his boss wasn't in the room right now, he quickly opened the app and read.

I'm in town.

James blinked. He had no idea what to make of that. *You mean in Gillham?*

Thankfully, Aaron answered right away. *Yes.*

Why was Aaron here? Why was he telling James? Did it mean he wanted to see James? James had a lot of questions, but he didn't think he could ask them right now. Things felt so fragile between them that he was terrified of pushing too hard, too fast. If he did, he would break something, and he would lose any chance he had to make something work with Aaron.

He stared at his phone, biting his lower lip. He didn't know why Aaron was telling him this, but he was no doubt waiting for something. *I'm at the bakery,* James typed.

I shouldn't have texted you, then. I'm sorry I bothered you.

James couldn't help but smile. *You didn't bother me. Why don't you come by? You don't have to if you don't want to, but I can't step away just now, and you could get a cupcake or whatever you like.*

James stared at the screen as he waited for Aaron to answer. He was pretty sure Aaron would say no. He had no idea where they stood or why Aaron was telling him about his presence in Gillham. It had to be because he wanted to see James, right?

"What are you doing?"

James jerked so hard he dropped his phone. "Jesus. I almost had a heart attack," he said, leaning down to pick up his phone and glaring at his boss.

Luckily for him, Al was a friend. There was no denying he was also James's boss, but they got along well, and Al never looked down at him.

Al arched a brow. "You know I don't want phones in this room. What would happen if you dropped it in one of the batters?"

James grimaced. "Sorry. It was important."

"Your family?"

James hesitated. Technically, Aaron wasn't his family, yet he also was. He was James's mate, and anyone would understand his need to make sure Aaron was okay. He hadn't told anyone about Aaron, though, but he supposed Al was as safe a person to tell as possible. "My mate."

Al blinked. "Aren't you too young to have a mate?"

James snorted. "Fate doesn't wait until you're thirty to throw your mate in your face. She certainly didn't in my case."

"You're only twenty, right?" Al asked as he leaned against the counter.

"And he's nineteen. It's a bit of a mess, honestly. He freaked out when he found out because he thought I would want to settle down right away. He didn't even talk to me. He just ran." It felt good to be talking to someone, especially someone who didn't have a stake in this. Al no doubt wanted James to be happy, but he wasn't as invested in that happiness as James's parents or his brothers were.

"Yet he's texting you?"

"We're trying to make something work between us, although what that something is, I'm not sure. He's not even from Gillham, which makes everything harder." James reached back and put his phone down on the counter without looking. Al's eyebrows rose on his forehead, but he didn't say anything. "I don't even know what I want from him. I guess I never really thought about it since I'm so young, even though it doesn't make sense. My brother met his mate, and he's about the same age as I am. I didn't think it would happen to me, though."

"And now you're overwhelmed. It explains why you were lost in your thoughts the past few days."

"I'm sorry. I know I haven't been focused."

Al shrugged. "Don't worry about it. It happens to everyone, but I'm glad I have an explanation. Why did he text you, then?"

"He's in town again. That's all he said, so I'm not sure he wants to see me. I told him to come by."

"You think he's going to come?"

"I don't know." James hoped so. As much as he told himself that he didn't care what Aaron decided and that he didn't need him in his life, he still *wanted* him in it.

It was ridiculous. James wasn't a romantic. He was a shifter, and he'd been told about mates since he was a child, but he'd never thought it was the best a shifter could get. He'd always wanted to focus on finding a job he loved, on doing something with his life, and he was doing it. Aaron had thrown a wrench into it, even though he didn't want James. James couldn't stop thinking about him, whether he wanted it or not.

"Well, let me know if you want to take some time off. It wouldn't be a problem for me."

James smiled. "Thank you. I have no idea what's going on, but I'm hoping that Aaron's texts mean he wants to at least talk to me."

"I hope the same." Al hesitated. "I know you're my employee, but I like you, James. I want you to succeed in life, and that includes in your personal life. Let me know if you need anything." He paused and grinned. "In the meantime, you're going to have to remake that dough."

James frowned and looked back. He swore when he saw he'd set his phone on top of the dough he'd been making. He snatched it, thankful it wasn't broken, but Al was right. He was going to have to remake the dough. "Dammit," he whined.

Al laughed and clapped him on the shoulder. "That's what

love does to us. It's a distraction, but it's the best distraction you'll ever have."

James wanted to tell him he wasn't in love with Aaron, but he knew it was only a matter of time.

That was, if Aaron gave him a chance to fall in love with him.

Aaron should have told James he was in town with both his fathers, but he hadn't thought about it, and now, it was too late. James expected him to go to the bakery, and Aaron wanted to. He wanted to see James again, but he hadn't told his fathers about him, and he didn't know how to do it.

They were in Gillham to talk to Bran, the head of the enforcers. Aaron was nervous about that and about his parents meeting James. He was going to have to explain who James was before they did, and he wasn't looking forward to it. They were going to be pissed that he hadn't told them as soon as he'd found James.

"Are you nervous?" Emery asked.

Aaron could only nod.

"He doesn't have a reason to be nervous," Nysys intervened. Everything is going to be perfect. He'll become an enforcer, and everyone will love him."

Aaron looked at him. "Why are you still here again?"

Nysys glared. "I'm here because I gave you and your fathers a ride. Well, a shimmer."

"And we're thankful," Emery intervened. "But we think this is a family matter. We'll call you as soon as we know what's going to happen."

Nysys scowled, but thankfully, he didn't start a fight. Aaron wasn't sure he could stand anything like that today. "Fine. Be like that. I wanted to support him, but if you want me to go home, I'll go." He smiled, apparently unable to help himself. "But really, Aaron. I wouldn't worry too much if I were you. You're going to be a great enforcer."

"I hope so," Aaron said, feeling a little choked up.

"And if you decide you don't want to be an enforcer, everyone will understand. I expect a phone call from all of you soon. I want to know what's going on. Aaron is my baby, too."

Aaron was pretty sure he saw Troy roll his eyes, but thankfully, Nysys didn't seem to notice. Either that, or he didn't comment on it.

He finally shimmered away, leaving Aaron and his parents in front of the house of the Gillham pack alpha. This was where they would be meeting Bran, and Aaron was nervous at the thought of meeting the alpha in this setting. He was used to Dominic, but he knew not everyone was like him. Kameron was a nice enough person when he visited Gillham, but this situation as different. What if he didn't want Aaron to be around, considering what Aaron was? It was one thing for Aaron to be far away in Whitedell, but having him in Gillham and in the enforcers would be very different.

A hand landed on Aaron's shoulder and squeezed. "It's going to be fine," Troy said.

"You can't know that."

"I can. Even if Bran decides you wouldn't be a good enforcer, you'll still have a home. You'll always have us, and we can help you find another job, something you love. I know you're worried but always remember that. We're not going anywhere, whatever you decide to do and whatever you end up doing."

Aaron couldn't do anything but nod. He was glad he'd made peace with his fathers. He should have talked to them from the beginning instead of waiting and letting things get as bad as they had. It was still hard, but they were trying to make time for him as well as his siblings, and he felt better. He was helping them take care of Hazel and Matthew, and he knew he should have done that from the beginning.

He was surprised his fathers were here, but maybe he shouldn't be. It had been easy to find a babysitter—there was always someone available with so many people living at the mansion in Whitedell. He wished James could be here, too, which didn't make sense. "Once this is over, I have to tell you something," he told his fathers.

Troy frowned. "Oh, boy. What else happened?"

Aaron should have been offended, but he couldn't be, not with the way he'd behaved the past few days. "Nothing bad. I promise. I should have told you sooner, but I was overwhelmed."

"As long as you're sure it's not anything bad."

"It's not. We can take care of it later." Hopefully, his parents would understand that he had no idea what to do with James. He could see them wanting to meet his mate, but he wasn't sure he was ready for that, or for anything else.

Troy wrapped an arm around Aaron's shoulders. "You can tell us anything. We should do this first, though. Bran is waiting for us."

He was. They didn't talk at the alpha's house, though. When they knocked and Bran answered, he stepped out, gesturing at the forest. "I thought Aaron would want to see the enforcers' building. It's not the same everywhere, but it will give him a good idea of where he would live, at least in the beginning."

Aaron was surprised. "You talk as if me being an enforcer is already a done deal."

Bran smiled at him. "On my side, it is. I don't see anything that would prevent you from becoming one."

Aaron swallowed. "Do you know what I am?"

"You mean a harpy shifter? I do, yes. You already know we don't have another harpy shifter, so you'll be a bit of a novelty. The enforcers will probably have a lot of questions, but

I'm sure your team will welcome you with open arms. Here, we don't care what you can shift into. As long as you work hard and have your team members' back, it's all that matters."

It sounded too good to be true. "And if I decide to do this, do you think I could be here in Gillham?"

Bran looked startled for a second. "Of course. I thought you would want to be in Whitedell, though."

Aaron didn't want to tell Bran about James in front of his parents, not when he hadn't told them yet. "I don't know. My family is in Whitedell, but my best friend is here. I guess I'll have to think about it."

Bran nodded. "You should, yes. If you truly want to do this, there's a place for you here or in Whitedell. I have a suggestion, though."

"Oh?" Aaron wasn't sure he was going to like it, but he was warming up to the idea of being an enforcer. If he decided to do this, he would be safer than if he'd hunted vampires on his own, and he would be able to choose where he wanted to live. His fathers would understand why he would pick Gillham as soon as he told them about James.

"It's something I offer to all recruits who aren't entirely sure they want to do this. You could shadow one of my teams for, let's say a few weeks. That way, you can see how they are together, how they work, what kind of missions they're sent on, things like that. Right now, you would mostly help clean up pack territory and the town after the fights we had to go through. It wouldn't be anything dangerous, but it would allow you to see what an enforcer's life is like."

"There's no danger that the town is going to be attacked again, right?" Troy asked.

He'd always been more worried about Aaron. Aaron thought it was because he felt guilty about passing on his harpy genes. Even after all these years, he still hadn't fully accepted that what he was wasn't his fault.

Bran shook his head. "We got rid of the Beasts, so they won't be a problem. Aaron would be safe here. Besides, he won't be alone. There will be an entire team with him, keeping an eye on him. Really, this is the best moment for him to do something like that."

The three of them turned to look at Aaron, and Aaron knew he had to give them an answer. He had nothing to lose by accepting. This way, he would see if being an enforcer was something he could deal with, and he would have time to spend with James. They would be in the same town for at least a while, and if Aaron decided to do this, they could be in the same town forever.

"I want to do it," he said, nodding.

Bran grinned. "Perfect. Let's meet your team, then."

James was arranging cupcakes in the glass counter when he heard the door open. He looked up, smiling to welcome the customers, and froze when he saw those customers were Aaron and two men who had to be his fathers.

James didn't know what to do. He couldn't look away, but he didn't know what Aaron wanted him to do. He was obviously flustered, gesturing as he spoke to his parents with flushed cheeks. Since this wasn't James's family, he decided to stay out of it. "Welcome," he said.

The shorter man smiled at him. "Thank you. Aaron told us you guys have great cupcakes."

James wasn't aware Aaron had ever eaten any of their cupcakes, but he was pleased. "I can get you a few. Just select them, and I'll bring them to your table."

The small tables by the wide window were one of the additions James had pushed for. Al had grumbled that he didn't see the need for them, but James had thought it would be nice for the customers to have a place to sit and eat their treats.

He'd been right. Usually, eating one cupcake led to the customers buying boxes of them, so Al hadn't been able to take the tables out, not when they were obviously useful. They also served coffee and tea, but nothing elaborate like the coffee shop.

The three men hovered by the counters for a few minutes, choosing their cupcakes. Aaron was trying to avoid looking at James, which was perfectly fine with James. Even though he wanted to know where he stood with Aaron, he also didn't want to rush his mate. He had the feeling that if he did, Aaron would run away again, and that this time, he would never come back. That meant he had to be careful and to give him space to do things at his pace. It was hard, but James would deal with it. Besides, he had enough to deal with himself. He still hadn't told his parents about Aaron, and he wasn't sure he should. He supposed he would find out soon enough.

Once the family had chosen their cupcakes, they headed to one of the tables. They'd also ordered coffee, so James got to work with that after poking his head in the back and telling Al about the customers. He was more than happy to let James deal with them.

James got a tray together, putting the cupcakes on three small plates, then headed toward them. He smiled as he put the tray down on the table and stepped back, but before he could leave, Aaron caught his wrist.

James sucked in a breath and looked at him.

"Aaron?" the bigger man asked. He sounded confused, and James was, too.

Aaron cleared his throat. "I wanted to introduce you. James, these are my parents, Troy and Emery."

James smiled at them, trying to ignore the way Aaron was still holding on to him. "It's a pleasure to meet you." He was glad to find out who was who. Aaron looked like Troy, with his red hair and freckles. They were both gorgeous, and James suspected that Troy was an image of the way Aaron would look once he was older. Emery was a gorgeous man, too. Aaron had his dark violet eyes. He was also slight like Emery, but tall like Troy.

"Dads, this is James. He's a wolf shifter, and he's my mate."

James's knees felt weak, but he stayed rooted in place. He stared at Aaron's parents, wondering how they would take it. Both of them were staring at James with wide eyes, so he was pretty sure Aaron had stunned them. That meant he hadn't told them before now, and James wasn't sure what to make of it.

"You didn't tell us you'd met your mate," Troy said.

Aaron shrugged. "I wanted to, but I wanted to fix things between us first. Besides, I wasn't nice to James, either."

Troy frowned. "I hope you fixed that, too."

"Not yet, but I'm going to." Aaron looked at James. "That is, if James lets me. I think we should talk."

James nodded numbly. "I can tell my boss I'm stepping away for a bit."

"Maybe later, once we're done here?"

"You know, I'm not surprised Aaron resisted the bond," Troy said before biting into his cupcake.

Aaron groaned. He'd finally let go of James, but James couldn't seem to be able to step away. He wasn't sure he should, either. Troy was clearly talking to him.

"I resisted, too," Troy explained when he saw James was staring. "Of course, my situation was different. I'd just been transformed into a half harpy, and I hated myself. When I met Emery, I was a mess. Things didn't get better once I found out I was pregnant, either. It took us a lot of work to make things work between us, but I'm sure you and Aaron will be able to do it, too."

"What if I hadn't told him that I could get pregnant?" Aaron asked.

"You clearly did since he's not running away screaming."

"Dad," Aaron whined. "Stop talking about that stuff. I ran away from James because I'm not ready to bond."

Troy reached out and patted Aaron's hand. "I wasn't ready, either. I still did it, and I never regretted it. That doesn't mean the two of you have to do it, though. Your situation is different, and I hope you'll take time to get to know each other."

"Why don't the two of you head out for a bit?" Emery suggested. "Troy and I could use some time alone."

James finally managed to move. He headed toward the back, poking his head through the door and telling Al he would be just outside. Al seemed amused, but he didn't try to stop him, thankfully.

Aaron was already outside when James turned back, and he strode through the store, nodding at Aaron's parents. Aaron looked up when he heard the door, and he smiled, looking embarrassed. "I'm sorry about what my dad said."

James shook his head. "Don't be. I'm happy to know we're not the only ones who had problems with the bond."

"But it's not the same. My father, well, he was a mess when he found out he'd been turned into a shifter, and especially a harpy shifter. Then he got pregnant with me, and everything was even worse. He even tried to cut me out of his body."

James's head was spinning, but he and Aaron were finally talking, and this was an important topic. He suspected they would talk about it again and again, and he would find out new details every time. "Can you really do that, too? I mean, get pregnant?" Aaron had already told James about it, but James had a hard time believing it.

Aaron hesitated. James expected him to refuse to answer, but instead, he nodded quickly. "In theory. I have the parts needed, like my father. Obviously, I've never tried. I know it's weird, and while I don't expect you to accept it. I can't do anything about it."

"You should expect me to accept it. It's part of you, and I would be an asshole if I didn't. But like you, I'm nowhere ready to settle down or to have children." Still, the thought that one day, they could create a life together was incredible—and terrifying. James did *not* want to think about that right now or anytime soon.

"Good, because neither am I. I'm going to be sticking around Gillham for a bit, though."

"Oh?"

"I talked with my parents about the vampire hunter thing. We agreed it's not the smartest idea, but my dad mentioned I could try becoming an enforcer. That's why we're in Gillham today. We went to talk to the head of the enforcers, and he suggested I spend some time with a team to see what the work is about."

"You didn't want to do that in Whitedell?" James knew there was several enforcers' teams there, too.

"I was hoping that by spending time here, you and I could talk things out and see if we can work things out."

James hadn't expected that, but he couldn't stop the smile from blooming on his face. "I'd like that."

Aaron smiled back. "Good. I'd like that, too."

Chapter Five

Aaron was nervous. He had half a mind to stay home, but he couldn't, not when his dads had done so much to provide him with this opportunity. Still, he obviously was the youngest on the team, and he was pretty sure the enforcers would treat him like a child.

Aaron eyed them as he waited for Bran to introduce him. He wished his parents could be there, but he wasn't a child, and he had to face this on his own. Still, it was the first time he would spend so much time away from home, and that didn't help keep him from getting nervous.

"Sue?" Bran called out.

One of the women turned to look at him. She arched a brow, but she got up from the couch and came closer.

They were in the enforcers' building in Gillham pack territory. Bran had explained that was where the enforcers, or at least, most of them, lived. Several were mated and had homes in town or in pack territory, but Aaron would be staying here, with the others. He was used to living with a lot of people, so that wouldn't be a problem. The problem was that he didn't know any of *these* people.

Sue looked at Aaron, clearly curious. "The entire team is here. I'm not sure why you thought moving Tanner to our team was a good idea, though. We already have a human."

Bran shook his head. "Things are up in the air right now with the town and pack territory needing cleaning up and fixing. You know I've been moving enforcers around. With so many of them finding mates and deciding to retire, it's getting hard to find enough people for teams. Besides, I think we've come a long way and that we don't need one representative of every kind of shifter and species in every team. It's easier to mix and match."

Aaron had no idea what they were talking about, and he wished they would stop. He needed to know what was going to happen next.

Bran put a hand on Aaron's shoulder. "And since your team is going to be staying in town for a bit, I thought it would be a good idea for Aaron to shadow you. He doesn't know whether or not he wants to become an enforcer yet, but this would be the easiest way for him to figure that out."

Sue turned her attention to Aaron again. She offered him her hand, and he shook it. "You want to become an enforcer, huh?"

Aaron shrugged, unsure of how to answer. "It's a thought I had."

"Well, you can stay with us for as long as you need to. Anything I need to know?"

Aaron sucked in a breath. He had to be honest, especially since Sue was going to be his team leader. "I'm nineteen, and I don't have experience in fighting or anything like that. There's also the fact that I'm a hybrid."

"You're not going to be doing any fighting, so that's not a problem. Can you expand on the hybrid thing?"

Aaron swallowed. "I think the entire team should probably be aware of what I am."

Sue stared at him for a moment before nodding. "Of course. Why don't you come to sit with us? We've been waiting for Bran and what he had to tell us, and I'm pretty sure that was you."

Bran squeezed Aaron's shoulder. "I can stay if you want," he said quietly.

Aaron shook his head. He did want Bran to stay because

he was the only one Aaron knew, but he had to do this alone. "I'll be fine."

"As long as you're sure."

"I am."

Once Bran was gone, Sue guided Aaron toward the rest of the team. They were sitting on couches and armchairs, talking to each other and clearly relaxed. They looked like a family, and it made Aaron's heart ache. Could he be part of that? Could he leave his own family behind to become an enforcer and be with his mate?

"Everyone, this is Aaron. He's going to be shadowing us for a bit while we help clean up the town. He wants to be an enforcer, but he wants to see what it's like before actually signing up for anything."

Several people nodded. A few waved at him, and Aaron awkwardly waved back. He might be used to being with a lot of people, but he'd never actually needed to be introduced to them. He'd always known everyone who lived in the mansion in Whitedell. They were his family, but these were strangers.

"Where are you from?" a man asked.

Sue knocked her shoulder against Aaron's. "That's Justin. He's a werewolf. He's mated and lives in town."

Aaron nodded and turned back to Justin. "I'm from Whitedell. I was born in the pride."

Justin beamed. "I remember you!"

Aaron frowned. He had no idea who Justin was. "You do?"

"I was an enforcer in Whitedell until I came here. I never mixed with the pride members, though. I had too much work as an enforcer. But I do remember seeing you around."

Fear gripped Aaron's guts. Did Justin know what he was? He forced himself to breathe. Even if Justin did, it didn't matter, since Aaron was about to tell these people. "I'm sorry, but I don't remember you."

Justin didn't look offended. "Figures. But it's not like we

spent any time together."

"Aaron has something to tell all of us," Sue intervened.

That got everyone's attention, and they stared at Aaron. He rubbed the back of his neck, realized what he was doing, and dropped his hand. "I just wanted all of you to know what kind of hybrid I am. There are only two of us as far as I know, and if I'm going to be part of your team, even if only temporarily, I think you ought to know."

"You don't have to tell us if it makes you uncomfortable," a woman said.

"I think I have to."

She frowned, but Sue cut her off when she opened her mouth again. "We can't push him either way, Rose. But I want Aaron to know that whatever he tells us, he's welcome with us. We don't have any kind of prejudice in this team."

Aaron felt reassured, but only slightly. He supposed he just had to say it and see what happened. "One of my fathers is a Krsnik. He's a kind of vampire and shifter hybrid, which means I am, too. My other father was human once, but he was experimented on, and now, he's a human-harpy hybrid." There. It was out, and now, Aaron only had to wait to see how to team would react.

Justin was slowly nodding. "I remember your fathers. Well, especially the harpy one. He has wings when he shifts, right?" Justin's expression lit up. "Do you? That would be so cool."

Aaron blinked. He'd expected rejection, or at the very least, disgust and mistrust. "I can actually shift into two forms."

"Jeesh," a huge man said. "Here I am, only human, and you can shift into two things?"

Aaron shrugged. "It's because of who my fathers are. I have a harpy form, which is me, but bigger and with wings, and a harpy eagle form, which comes from my Krsnik father." Aaron didn't want to tell them that he could also get pregnant. He had no intention of letting that happen anytime soon, and they didn't need to know that to keep him safe or to make sure he could help them if anything happened. That was one secret he was more than happy to keep.

"Well, now that we all know each other," Sue started.

Another man interrupted her. "But we don't. We know who Aaron is, but he has no idea who most of us are."

Sue glared at him and pointed. "Fine. That's Lorcan. He's a falcon shifter, so maybe the two of you can fly together." She continued pointing at the people in the room. "That's Davis. He's a bear. You already know Rose and Justin, and that's Janelle. The big one who complained about being human is Xander, and those two are Nadha and Tanner. You can have a chat with all of them and find out what they can shift into and what they can do. You have time." She clapped her hands together. "As Bran explained the other day, most of the teams are going to stay in town and help clean up and make sure everyone is fine. That means us, too. Be ready to head out in an hour."

Several people groaned, but Aaron was excited. He had no idea what was going to happen, but he felt good about how the team had welcomed him.

He'd always thought that what he was would be an obstacle. He'd thought people would hate him for it or be disgusted. Instead, the team had seemed envious of the fact that he could shift into two different forms. They'd accepted it without a problem, and that gave Aaron hope.

Every step took him closer to being happy and having a good life, and he couldn't wait to see what the next one would bring.

James knew today was the day Aaron had met the enforcers' team he would be shadowing for a while. Aaron hadn't called him or answered his texts, and he was trying hard not to be offended. No doubt his mate had a lot of things to do and focus on and answering James would be a distraction. Still, it was evening now, and there was still no sign of Aaron. James knew the enforcers' team worked long hours, but this long?

"What's going on?" Lee asked, knocking their shoulders together.

James was out with Lee, Telyn, and a few other friends. He hadn't been sure it was a good idea, but he'd wanted something to distract himself. Unfortunately, it wasn't working.

"Nothing," he told his brother, forcing himself to smile.

"You know I can see you're lying, right?"

James sighed. "I'm just thinking about Aaron."

Lee slowly nodded. "How is that going?"

"I honestly have no idea."

"I thought the two of you talked."

"We did, and we agreed to get to know each other, but it hasn't been easy. He still has a lot to fix with his parents, and he's terrified that I want more than he's ready to give."

"Well, nothing is going to solve that except talking to him."

"I was hoping we could soon. He's in Gillham right now. He's spending time with the enforcers."

Lee looked surprised. "It's good he doesn't want to be a hunter anymore. At least you know he's not going to be alone out there getting himself killed."

"It is."

"But you were hoping he'd call you tonight. He's in the same town as you, yet you haven't heard from him."

James glared at his brother. "How do you know I haven't?"

"It's kind of obvious." His gaze drifted behind James, who was sitting with his back to the door. "Maybe you'll have the opportunity to talk to him sooner than you think."

James twisted in his chair. The door of the bar was open, and people were streaming in. They weren't wearing their enforcer uniforms, but James knew them by sight. Aaron was with them. He was talking with one of the men, and he didn't look up as he entered.

James hesitated. He wanted to talk to his mate, but he also didn't want to interrupt him. Even if Aaron never became part of this team, it would be good to make friends with the enforcers. If he was going to do this, he needed people at his back.

James turned back to Lee. "At least I know he's okay," he said.

"You're not going to talk to him?"

"I don't think he would thank me for that. He's here to spend time with the enforcers and decide whether or not it's something he can see himself doing in the future. I don't want to interrupt him."

Lee didn't look convinced, but thankfully, he didn't push.

A hand on James's shoulder made him jump. He twisted again, his eyes widening when he saw Aaron standing next to him. "I didn't know you'd seen me," he said.

Aaron smiled. "How could I not see you? I noticed you as soon as I stepped in."

James nodded. He wasn't sure what to say. "You're here with your team."

Aaron briefly looked at them. They were sitting at a table close by, and a few of them were looking at Aaron and James. "They're not my team yet, and I don't know if they'll ever be."

"But you're friendly with them."

"They welcomed me. I didn't expect it, and it's nice."

James took a moment to look at his mate. Every time they'd seen each other, Aaron had been tense about one thing or another. Tonight, though, he was relaxed. "Well, you shouldn't keep them waiting."

Aaron looked at James again. "I thought I could sit with you and your friends. I'm going to be spending a lot of time with the team. I think it's time I spend more time with you, too."

James couldn't say no to that. He was grateful when Lee grabbed a chair from a table nearby and dragged it closer, then moved his own closer to Telyn's. He nodded at Aaron, and Aaron nodded back. James hoped that they would become friends in time, but he could see it was going to take some work. Lee was offended by what Aaron had put James through, and he wouldn't give in easily.

Aaron slid into the chair. He was so close to James that James could feel his warmth through their clothes. James shook himself and introduced him to Telyn, Brandon, and Maddox. They all were curious, but thankfully, they didn't ask who Aaron was.

"I wanted to apologize," Aaron said, leaning even closer to James.

"What for?"

"For the way I treated you, especially when we met, but today, too. I should have found the time to answer at least one of your texts."

"You make it sound like I sent you a hundred." It had only been two, and James hoped it wasn't too many.

"I still should have taken a few moments to answer. I was kind of overwhelmed, especially after the team started working. I'm sorry." He hesitated, then, to James's surprise, he reached for James's hand and took it. "I'm even more sorry for running away from you and treating you badly when we met. I was angry and lost, and in a way, I still am. I'm working on it, though. It's not easy, but I do hope it will give us a chance to get to know each other, and maybe eventually, to be together."

James tried not to hope too much. He wanted to believe Aaron, but he was still afraid. Even if Aaron was working on himself and his problems, it didn't mean he'd want James in his life or that he wouldn't change his mind.

Aaron smiled crookedly. "I can see you don't believe me, but that's fine. I have time to convince you."

James shook his head. "It's not that I don't believe you. I want to."

"But I was an asshole, and you want to make sure you don't get hurt. That's fine. Just give me a chance, and I'll work with that."

James nodded as he looked around. He was the only single guy at the table. He'd noticed it, of course, but no one had said anything about it. It had been obvious, though. Lee had Telyn, and Brandon had Maddox. James hadn't had anyone—until now.

"How was your first day?" he asked. Since Aaron was making an effort, James had to do the same. He wanted to get to know his mate. Whatever happened between them, it couldn't erase the bond that linked them together. They would always be mates, and he wanted Aaron to know that it meant something to him.

Aaron leaned back in his chair. "It wasn't what I expected."

James chuckled. "You thought you'd get to kick ass?"

That made Aaron laugh. "I was warned I wouldn't, so no. And I didn't mind help cleaning up the town. It was kind of horrifying to see what the Beasts put Gillham through. No, what surprised me was the team."

"How come?"

Aaron looked at their hands.

They were still twined together, and neither of them had given any sign they wanted to stop. James certainly didn't.

"I expected them to push me away. The people in my life have always accepted me, but it's because they've known me since I was born. They've always known what kind of hybrid I was. I was terrified that when I told the team about it, they would push me away because I was a freak."

"You're not a freak," James said. He could hear from Aaron's voice that he'd been called that too many times.

"I know. But when I told my friends at school what I was, that's what they called me. It was easier to be homeschooled, which is what I did, at least for a while. I've always been afraid of making friends. I think it's part of the reason I pushed you away. I couldn't *not* tell the team, though. I have to know they'll have my back if something happens, and they have to know I have theirs, even though so far, we've only been cleaning up. But if I'm going to become an enforcer, I can't hide what I am anymore. The thought of telling people was always terrifying, and today wasn't any different."

"But they welcomed you with open arms."

"They did. It gives me hope."

It gave James hope, too. It was going to take time for Aaron to deal with his insecurities, but this was the first step to make it happen. James hoped he would be there to see the rest.

Aaron was flustered, which was ridiculous. He'd had boyfriends. Not a lot of them, since he was always afraid to tell them what he was—and a few hadn't taken it well—but he'd had crushes, and he knew what to do. This felt like the first time he was in love, though, and it made him scowl at his own reaction. He'd wanted to be relaxed, to appear as if he didn't care, but he did. He wanted James to like him, something he knew would be hard, considering how he'd behaved. He was babbling, and he hoped James wouldn't hold it against him. He didn't think so, but he was still wary of James and everyone else. He didn't know them well yet, and they could still change their mind about him.

Besides, James was different. He wasn't just a crush or a boyfriend. He was Aaron's mate. Aaron was still offended that James would have given him up so easily, and he couldn't help but bring it up as the conversation drifted. "The day we talked at Adam's house," he started, unsure how to continue.

James smiled at him. "You're still offended, aren't you?"

"How did you know?"

James shrugged. "You looked offended then, like you didn't understand why I would want to be with someone else."

"I still don't. We're mates, and you said it was important, yet you looked ready to be with anyone but me."

James shook his head and reached for his soda with his free hand. So far, he hadn't given any inclination that he didn't want Aaron to hold his other hand, but Aaron expected that to happen eventually. He expected a lot of things to go wrong with James, even though so far, they hadn't. "I was trying to look stronger than I felt," James eventually said.

"I'm sure you're very strong."

"Maybe. But you were telling me you didn't want me, and I wanted you to know that even without you, I would be fine. It wouldn't have been easy, though."

"You made it sound like it."

"You shouldn't believe everything I say. I wanted to appear strong, even though I was breaking inside." He swallowed and licked his lips. "We're way too young to bond, and I know that."

"Adam and Sterling are bonded," Aaron pointed out.

"And it was right for them. It wouldn't be right for us, though. You have a lot of problems to solve, and I'm too hesitant to trust you."

That hurt more than it should have. It was all Aaron's fault, though, and he only had himself to blame for James not trusting him. "I understand."

"I don't think you do. Or maybe you do, I don't know. I would have been happy to talk to you and just get to know each other, but you pushed me away from the beginning. I thought something was wrong with me. I have my own insecurities, I guess."

Aaron squeezed his hand. "Everyone has insecurities."

James nodded and squeezed back. "I was trying to protect myself when I told you that I could live without you. I mean, I know I would have managed. Even though we're mates, we're not bonded, and eventually, I could have found someone else. I'm only twenty, and I have time. It wouldn't have been easy, though. I didn't want to push you, and I thought that was the best way not to."

"As much as I hate that I hurt you, I think you reacted the only way that made sense. If you'd pushed to have something with me, I would have panicked, and I would have run away."

James arched a brow. "You won't run away now?"

Aaron hesitated. He wanted to say he wouldn't, but could he? "I can't make any promises. Sometimes I'm still terrified, both by you and by everything else. Things might be going better, but it doesn't mean all my problems are solved. I have a lot of work to do. What I can promise you is that I won't be a dick again. I don't know what the future will be like, for me or for us together, but I want to give us a chance."

Aaron's heart raced in his chest. He hadn't come here tonight to tell James he wanted him. He hadn't even known James would be there. The team had wanted to get a drink with him, even though he was only nineteen. They'd insisted that he could stick with soda and no one would care. But when Aaron had seen James, he'd known he would spend the evening with his mate. He felt drawn to him, and he wanted to get to know him. No one in the team had minded. A few had teased him about having heart eyes, but he hadn't cared. Maybe he did have heart eyes.

He didn't know James well, but he wanted that to change.

He truly wanted to see if they could work as mates. He was relieved that James was nowhere near ready to bond, just like he wasn't, and that they had time. He was in Gillham now, and it would give them opportunities to spend time together and see if they could make things work.

And they could. Aaron already knew that. He and James were mates for a reason.

Maybe that was why he'd met James now. Maybe he'd needed James to show him how stupid he was being and to give him the kick in the butt he needed to start working on himself and solving his problems.

They'd been invented problems to begin with. Aaron had felt abandoned, lonely, and lost, but he could have solved everything by talking to his parents. He could have helped them with the kids more and given them more time to relax and be able to listen to him. Instead, he'd dug his heels in and continued acting like a brat.

That was over now. He couldn't promise he would never act childish again, but he was only nineteen. He suspected most people expected him to continue being an asshole, at least sometimes. He would show everyone he could change, though. He *wanted* to change. He wanted to be a good son to his fathers and a good mate to James, eventually. He wanted to become a good enforcer. He wanted to be a better friend to Adam.

And he was the only one who could make all that happen.

James was clearly still hesitant to give him a chance, but Aaron knew he had to push at least a bit. "You're not ready to bond, and neither am I. I'm going to have to spend a lot of time focusing on becoming an enforcer and training, but I still want to see you and talk to you during that time," he said. "I want both of us to give this a chance. I know you're afraid. We both are. What if I promise that if something is wrong, I'll talk to you?"

"Instead of flying away?"

Aaron rubbed the back of his neck with his free hand. "That wasn't the best way to react to finding out we were mates."

James snorted. "Can you really promise to tell me if something is wrong?" he asked.

"I have a lot of changes to make, and I'm aware of that. It's hard, but I need to make all of them happen, including with you. I can't promise I'll be the perfect mate, but I sure as hell am going to try."

"So you want things between us to work?"

Aaron nodded. "I want us to have a chance and to work toward being together, and eventually, bonding and having a family. Years from now, of course," he added in a rush.

"You were terrified by the idea only days ago."

"I was. But I realized that I don't have to do everything at once. I'm only nineteen. As my parents said, I have all the time in the world to make decisions, and even once I do, I can change my mind. Both of us are going to live for a long time. We don't have to rush into anything, and knowing that helps."

Aaron knew his cheeks were pink, and he had to fight the urge to look away from James. James deserved to hear all of this, though. He deserved Aaron's promises, and Aaron had every intention of keeping them.

James wanted to believe Aaron so freaking much. Now that he'd gotten over the bitterness of Aaron running away from him the night they'd met, he could see how much Aaron appealed to him. His wolf had been half in love with Aaron since the first time they'd seen each other, even though James had never given it much thought. James had been reluctant, and he still was. It was hard when Aaron was so flustered, though. His cheeks had reddened, and that looked so good with his red hair and freckles. His eyes were odd, but in the best of ways. James had never seen violet eyes, and he'd expected Aaron's eyes to be green, since he was a redhead. They weren't, and he found himself leaning closer to get a better look.

He caught himself before he could make a fool of himself and moved back. He had to be careful with his heart. He wanted to believe Aaron, but he wasn't sure he could. Aaron was saying all the right things, and maybe he meant them. He sure looked like he did.

James had to give him a chance. If they wanted things to work between them, they couldn't go on the way they'd been. They had to move forward instead of backward, and that was what Aaron was trying to do. James could make things hard for both of them, but he didn't want to.

He was going to make sure Aaron didn't hurt him, but he was also going to give him a chance.

He finally nodded, and he saw how much Aaron relaxed. "All right," James said.

"You're going to have to be more specific. What are you saying all right to?"

Aaron looked nervous. James wasn't sure why he was surprised. Aaron wanted a relationship with him, even though they'd started on the wrong foot, and he didn't know what James was agreeing to. "We can give this a try. I know being mates is daunting, but we don't have to rush into anything. We can get to know each other and see what happens." It was going to be even easier now that Aaron was in town. James felt lighter. This was what he'd wanted, and even though he was still skeptical, he wouldn't let that emotion take over. He and Aaron had a chance at something great, just like what Lee and Telyn had. James wasn't going to allow that to slip from his fingers just because he was stubborn.

They spent the rest of the evening together. Aaron looked

at the enforcers a few times and even went over to them once, but he always returned to James. James wasn't sure if it was because he wanted to or because he was drawn to him as his mate, but he didn't think it mattered.

No matter how much they both wanted to separate who they were from their bond, it wasn't possible. They couldn't ignore it, because it changed the way they behaved with each other. It made them push against each other, move closer, and now, James found it hard to stop.

That was why when they finally left the bar after a few hours, he offered Aaron a ride. "I don't know where you're staying, but I can drive you anywhere."

"I have a room in the enforcers' building," Aaron said.

His cheeks were still flushed, making James want to reach out for him. He almost did just that, but the bar door opened, and a group of laughing people spilled out, interrupting them. "I can take you. I live in pack territory anyway."

Aaron looked pleased. They held hands as they walked toward the car. It was strange, but it also felt good. James hadn't thought he and Aaron would have this. For a while, it had looked like they wouldn't. Aaron had come back, though, and James's heart beat faster every time he thought about his mate.

Did it really matter that neither of them was ready to bond? They wouldn't be the only ones. Lee and Telyn had bonded, and so had Adam and Sterling, but their circumstances were different. Telyn had needed to be shown that Lee truly cared for him and wouldn't abandon him, while Adam had wanted to be there for Sterling and his siblings after their parents had died. Aaron and James didn't have a reason to bond as quickly, which was good. James wanted to take his time and make sure he was ready before anything like that happened, especially with the knowledge that Aaron could get pregnant.

That was probably something they would have to talk

about sooner rather than later. Even if they weren't ready to bond, it didn't mean James didn't want to get Aaron into bed—or on any flat surface. He was a young adult, after all.

He hesitated to talk about it when they got into the car, but he supposed he might as well get it out of the way. With how things were going, he fully expected to kiss Aaron tonight and to do something more soon. That was, if Aaron was okay with it.

"What do you think about sex?" he blurted out. He regretted the words as soon as they were out of his mouth, but he couldn't take them back. At least he couldn't see Aaron well in the darkness.

"I like it."

James let out a breath. "Good. I mean, I like it too."

He could hear the humor in Aaron's voice when Aaron answered. "I guess we're well suited, then. Did you want to know anything specific about me and sex?"

"Well, you said you could get pregnant, and that your father didn't know that when he got pregnant with you. I guess we should talk about that."

Aaron sighed. "You're right. We should. I wish we didn't have to, because it's not exactly first-date conversation, but we're mates. You're in my life for the long haul. So, I take contraceptives. I was lucky that once people realized what happened to my father and that he could get pregnant, they started working on contraceptives that would work on him. He's been taking them for years. It also means that as soon as I was old enough to have sex, my father sat me down and asked me if I wanted to take them. I said yes. I'm nowhere near ready to have children. I'm not sure I'll ever be."

"We don't have to talk about kids right now. I just wanted to know…" James wasn't sure how to finish that sentence.

"You wanted to know if you could fuck me without getting me pregnant."

James spluttered, but that was *exactly* what he'd wanted to know. "We don't have to do anything you're not ready for. Besides, it's not going to be easy. I still live with my parents, and right now, you live with a bunch of people."

"There's more to sex than penetration. Trust me. I have experience with that. Even though I was taking the pill, I was terrified I would get pregnant anyway. I've only had that kind of sex a few times."

This wasn't the way James had expected the conversation to go, but he was glad they were having it. It was a sign they were both more adult than he'd thought. "Okay, so how about we agree not to have penetrative sex until we can take our time and be careful?"

"I don't know. Does this mean we can't have sex at all until we have the perfect place and moment?"

"God, no," James blurted out. When Aaron chuckled, James continued, "I want to have sex with you. Even when I didn't know you personally, I would see you around sometimes, and I always thought you were sexy as fuck."

"I'm your type, then?"

"I'm pretty sure you're everyone's type, but the fact that you're my mate helps."

James wasn't sure what to think about the fact that the conversation stopped after that. He supposed they both had a lot to think about. It had to be terrifying to know that you could get pregnant if you weren't careful, especially after Aaron's father had gone through that. James had never had to deal with that problem. He was gay, and he'd never been with a girl.

He was working himself into a tizzy by the time he stopped in front of the enforcers' building. A lot of windows were still lit up, and he made sure to park at the far end of the lot. He had no idea what was about to happen, but just in case, he wanted them to have at least a bit of privacy.

He turned off the engine, unhooked his seatbelt, and twisted in his seat to look at Aaron.

Aaron was looking back at him.

His eyes glinted in the darkness. James could see more of him now that they were in front of the house, and he wanted to reach for him again. He wondered if that would ever stop. He supposed not, since they were mates and they were supposedly perfect for each other and all that. So far, they didn't seem to be, but that would change.

"What now?" he murmured.

"What do you want to do? I can go to my room, and we'll see each other tomorrow."

"What's the alternative?"

Aaron grinned. "The alternative is that we could stay in the car for a bit longer."

He reached for James at the same time James reached for him. They met in the middle, their lips pressing against each other. It was awkward for a few moments, both of them fumbling to find a way to make their faces and lips fit together. The car wasn't the perfect place to do this, especially considering how small it was, but they made it work.

They had to.

Aaron tried to scramble closer to James, but he hit the roof with his head. He yelped and jerked back, rubbing the sore spot. "Maybe staying in the car wasn't such a good idea."

He looked so good with his parted lips glistening, and James was sure that he was also blushing. He wanted more of that. He wanted more of *Aaron*, period.

Aaron was taller than James, which meant James had to be the one doing this. After seeing what had happened to Aaron, he was careful, but he managed to turn around and straddle his mate's lap. Aaron's hands landed on James's hips, and when James leaned closer, he could see how wide Aaron's eyes were.

"Still okay?" he murmured.

Aaron nodded enthusiastically. "I promise I'll tell you if something isn't."

"I'll do the same."

Then they were kissing again, and this time, they didn't stop.

It felt good, much better than it had with anyone else James had ever kissed. He knew it was because of the bond, or maybe because he was horny. Whatever the reason, he never wanted this to stop, and he hoped he and Aaron would manage to make things work. He wanted more now, though, and since Aaron had promised he would stop him if he did anything Aaron didn't want, he decided to take a risk. After all, Aaron had said he liked sex. Maybe he wouldn't be opposed to them getting frisky in the car.

James pushed his hand between them without moving away from Aaron. He didn't want to stop kissing him, just to get to him more easily. They were both wearing jeans, though. He fumbled around for a bit, unable to undo Aaron's with only one hand. Luckily for him, Aaron seemed to know what he was doing, and he decided to help. After trying to get each other's jeans open, they gave up and moved on to opening their own. It was faster and more efficient, which was what James wanted right now.

James breathed in relief when his cock was finally free. He was glad Aaron couldn't see him well in the darkness. He knew he looked okay, but he was still hesitant. He supposed it was normal, even though he didn't like it much.

Then every thought about Aaron seeing his naked body flew out of his mind, because Aaron reached for his cock. He wrapped his fingers around it, pulling on the skin and making James pant. This wasn't how James had imagined their first time, but that didn't mean it wasn't perfect.

He reached for Aaron, pushing their lips together again as

he thrust his hips forward. Aaron groaned, and they had to wiggle so they could find a more comfortable position.

Together, they managed to wrap their fingers around their cocks. James's arm was twisted, but he didn't care. The only thing he cared about right now was the pleasure building in his groin and the way Aaron felt under him. The air smelled of sex, and Aaron made adorable little groans and moans that James wanted more of.

To his surprise, he also wanted to bite Aaron's neck.

He knew it was his wolf pushing for it, and he did his best to ignore it. He couldn't afford to make that kind of mistake, and he didn't want to. From the way Aaron kept peeking at his neck, James was pretty sure he felt the same way. Now that he was this close to his mate, he could see the fangs in Aaron's mouth, and as adorable as they were, he wasn't looking forward to having them sink into his neck, not anytime soon.

James kissed Aaron again so neither of them would have the temptation to bite. Aaron's fangs scraped against James's tongue, making him shudder in pleasure. At the same time, Aaron did something with his hand, twisted it to the side and upward, and that was it for James.

He'd wanted things to last longer, but he couldn't stop himself from coming. Aaron felt too good under him. He groaned, biting Aaron's lower lip, hoping that was okay. Aaron pushed against him, and James thought he was smiling. That didn't last long, though, because as soon as James was done coming, he focused on his mate. He was easier to do now, and within moments, Aaron was coming, too, shuddering against James and whimpering into his mouth.

They were both breathing hard. James took a moment to try to relax, but now that they were done, he could feel all the aches and pains from having sex in the car. He didn't think he could stay in this position for much longer, and he groaned as he leaned away.

"Are you okay?" Aaron asked.

James kissed him before swinging himself back into the driver's seat. He stretched, smiling languidly. "I'm perfect."

"I'm that good, huh?"

James reached out and gently slapped the back of Aaron's head. "Don't let your head swell."

"My head isn't the thing that swelled just now."

"That was terrible." But James was looking forward to many more terrible jokes from Aaron. He was looking forward to a lot when it came to Aaron, and for the first time, he really felt like they could make it.

Chapter Six

If anyone had told Aaron his life would be like this, he wouldn't have listened to them. He'd been so focused on the negative parts of his life, on feeling like he didn't belong and like his parents had abandoned him, that he'd barely thought about the good parts. Now, he couldn't stop thinking about them.

He loved living and working with the enforcers. They felt like a second family, even though he wasn't sure he would be able to stay here if he decided to make it a job. Everything they did was simple, like cleaning up pack territory and the town, but it made Aaron feel useful, something he hadn't realized he needed until now.

He missed his dads and even his siblings, but they texted and called, and they visited each other as often as possible. Luckily for them, it wasn't hard to shimmer back and forth between Whitedell and Gillham.

And of course, there was James. Aaron and James had been talking almost every day. After what had happened in the car, Aaron couldn't wait for more, but he and James were careful. Neither of them wanted to get hurt or to hurt the other. That meant Aaron still had no idea what would happen with James, but he didn't need to. They were both young. They had time to make decisions, fall in love, and do everything that came with that.

Not that it was going to take much time for Aaron to fall in love with James. He was pretty sure he was already halfway there, and for the first time, it didn't terrify him. He wouldn't say he was comfortable with the feeling, but he would have freaked out if this had happened a month ago. As it was, he was waiting to see what was next between them. He'd already decided he would stop fighting. He and James were mates for a reason, just like they'd met now for a reason. Aaron didn't know what the reason was, and he might never find out, but he did know that now that he had James in his life, he wasn't giving him up.

He couldn't stop smiling as he walked to the bakery to pick up his mate. His heart raced, just like every time he spent time with James. He hadn't known it would be so easy to fall in love. He'd wanted to push back, to avoid it as much as possible, but that was impossible when it came to James. James had broken down all the walls Aaron had erected around his heart. He'd been terrified to trust someone, afraid James would think he was a freak and would push him away, but instead, James had welcomed him with open arms.

Well, mostly. James was obviously hesitant, too, and Aaron didn't blame him, after the way he'd treated him in the beginning. It was something they were working on, and Aaron hoped that James would trust him in time.

They were still way too young to bond, and neither of them had even mentioned it. Aaron felt the need to run away if he thought about it, but instead, he continued walking to the bakery. He was picking up James after work, and he was taking him on a date.

Aaron even loved Gillham. It was similar to Whitedell, but here, not everyone knew him. It felt good to be invisible, which was one of the reasons he was tempted to ask Bran if he could move to Gillham permanently. He wanted to talk to his fathers about it first, though. They wouldn't try to stop him, but they wouldn't be happy to lose him, even though it wouldn't be true loss.

Aaron's phone rang in his pocket just before he got to the

bakery. He looked through the window, but he couldn't see James anywhere, because he usually worked in the back. He was a few minutes early, so he took out his phone and answered. "Yes?"

"Are you ever coming back?" Nysys asked.

Aaron sighed. "What do you want?"

"I just told you what I wanted. An answer."

"I don't know. I'm working, though. I can't just dump everything and come to you because you did something. Call someone else."

"I never said I needed anything. I just miss you."

Aaron rolled his eyes. "Sure you do."

"It's the truth. I do miss you, and I know I'm not the only one. So? Are you coming back or not?"

Aaron hesitated. "Maybe."

Nysys tsked. "Not at all, from what you're saying."

"I didn't say that."

"You didn't have to. Your fathers have been closed-lipped about what you're doing in Gillham."

"Didn't they mentioned I'm working with the enforcers?" It wasn't a secret, so Aaron hadn't asked his fathers to keep quiet about it. Besides, Nysys knew about it, which meant the entire pride did, too.

"Yes, but most of us don't know why you're in Gillham instead of in Whitedell. It would have made more sense. That's why I think you're hiding something."

"That's why you called, isn't it? You want to find out my secret."

"Are you going to tell me?" Nysys sounded excited.

Aaron wasn't surprised. Everyone knew there was little Nysys liked more than secrets, and one of those things was to know secrets before anyone else.

"I just wanted to spend time with Adam."

Nysys snorted. "Don't lie to me. I'm a professional liar, and

I smell lies from miles away."

Aaron hesitated. He wasn't sure that telling Nysys was the best idea, but he wouldn't mind having someone to talk to. He could talk to his parents, but they were biased. They wanted Aaron to be happy, even if it meant he would move to Gillham permanently. The same went for Adam. Adam wanted Aaron close, and Aaron couldn't deny he wanted to spend more time with his friend, too.

"Fine. There's a reason I'm here," he confessed.

"I *knew* it. Come on. Tell me what it is."

"You're not going to tell anyone, though."

"I know how to keep secrets."

Aaron wasn't convinced. "Do you?"

"If I have to, yes. So? What's going on?"

It still felt strange to confess to someone who wasn't his parents that he had a mate. "I met someone," he started, unsure how to continue.

"Of course you did. Isn't that how things always go?"

"I don't know. Do you want to hear about it? Or would you rather talk over me?"

"I'm all ears. I promise I won't interrupt again."

Aaron doubted it, but he didn't have a choice, not if he wanted Nysys's advice. "This someone isn't just a guy. He's my mate."

Nysys screeched, and Aaron had to move the phone away from his ear. He waited for a few seconds, then pressed it against his ear again. Nysys was still making noise and cooing, and Aaron didn't have much time. "Are you done?" he asked.

"Little Aaron found his mate. I can't believe it."

"Don't call me little."

"You'll always be little to me. I changed your diapers when you were a kid."

"You don't have to remind me every time I ask you for

advice."

"I'm not sure what you're asking me, to be honest."

"I don't know if I should stay in Gillham permanently. My mate is here, and he's not moving, but my entire life is in Whitedell."

"Part of your life is in Gillham now."

"Having to make this decision is terrifying."

"All the big decisions are terrifying. They wouldn't be big decisions if they weren't. You already know what to do, though. You don't need my advice."

He was right. Aaron did know what to do.

Aaron looked up, and just then, James walked into the bakery's main area, holding a tray. Aaron couldn't look away, and he found he didn't want to. He'd already made his decision. He didn't need to ask Nysys or anyone for advice. There was only one thing he could do, and he was already doing it.

He was going to move to Gillham to be with James. It was scary, but it also felt like the right thing to do, and Aaron knew he wouldn't regret it. James was his future, while Whitedell was his past. He could only look forward, and he had every intention of doing just that.

James had noticed Aaron outside the bakery, but he continued working since Aaron was on the phone. He could see Aaron peeking at him every so often, and he had to resist the urge to wave at him. Whoever Aaron was talking to, it looked serious, and James didn't want to intrude.

He kept an eye on his mate until Aaron hung up, took a deep breath, and moved toward the bakery door. Then James couldn't stop smiling.

"Who's that?" Al asked.

"My mate." It felt good to say it, and now, James could.

Al blinked. "I still think you're too young to have a mate."

"That's why we're taking things slow. There's no saying when you meet your mate, though. I suppose Aaron and I were lucky we met so young."

"As long as you're happy. You should go in the back and wash up. He's picking you up?"

"We're going on a date."

Al looked James up and down. "Then you should *definitely* clean up. You have a streak of flour on your cheek."

James reached up and scrubbed it just as Aaron stopped in front of the counter. James's smile softened, and he dropped his hand. "Hi," he said.

Aaron smiled back. "Hi."

They stood staring at each other until Al grunted. "I swear, young people these days," he grumbled.

James laughed. "You talk as if you're eighty."

"Some days, I feel like I am. Go clean up. I'm sure your boyfriend won't have a problem waiting for you here."

James was glad Al hadn't called Aaron his mate. They might be mates, but they were still trying to become comfortable with being called that.

James smiled at Aaron one last time, then went to the back room. He cleaned up as best and quickly as he could, not wanting to make Aaron wait. When he got back to the main area, he was surprised to find Aaron and Al talking. They stopped when he arrived, and Aaron turned his attention to him.

He looked nervous. He kept pulling on his jacket and looking around as if he was looking for an escape. James hoped he wasn't going to run away a second time. He wasn't sure he could stand that.

"Ready?" Aaron asked.

James nodded. "Ready."

They left after saying their goodbyes to Al, and James waited until they were out of sight of the bakery to turn to

Aaron. "Everything okay?" he asked.

"Yes."

"I saw you on the phone earlier, and it looked serious."

"It wasn't. It was Nysys."

James had heard about Nysys from several pack members. Apparently, he was quite famous. James had no idea why, but the man seemed to be odd. "Is he one of your friends?"

"Not really. It's weird, because he changed my diapers and babysat me when I was a kid. Our relationship changed as I grew up, and now, I guess we're kind of friends?"

"Well, that's good. What did he want?"

Aaron shrugged. His cheeks were flushed, and he kept looking around. It was almost as if he didn't want to talk about this. "He called and asked me if I was coming back," Aaron finally said.

They hadn't talked about this yet. Aaron was working with the enforcers, and he seemed to be having fun and loving what he was doing, but they both knew it was only temporary. Eventually, Aaron would have to make a decision, and while James knew what *he* wanted, he wouldn't be the one to decide.

"What did you say?" James asked cautiously.

Aaron sighed. "I asked him what I should do."

"And what did he answer?" James held his breath. He and Aaron could make things work if Aaron went back to Whitedell, but James didn't want that to happen. He wanted Aaron to be close by. He wanted them to be able to see each other often.

"That I already knew what I should do. And he was right. I know what I want and what I should do. I just need the courage to do it."

"Are you going to tell me?" James suspected Aaron was going to leave, maybe become an enforcer in Whitedell. It would make sense. since his family was there. James was his mate, but they'd decided to take things slow, and putting some distance between them would make that work better. As it was, it was hard to remember they weren't ready to bond when they were together. Aaron was perfect, or at least, perfect for James.

"I want to be an enforcer," Aaron said. "I think it's definitely going to be better than hunting vampires on my own."

"That's a relief. Have you talked to Bran yet?"

"No, and I haven't talked to my parents, either. They won't be pleased that I decided to stay here, but they'll understand, and they won't try to stop me."

James sighed in relief. "So you want to be an enforcer here in Gillham?"

"Ideally, yes. I know Bran can move enforcers around, but I hope he'll agree to have me do this in Gillham once I tell him about you. I'm sure we could make it work either way, but I don't want to leave you behind."

James shouldn't have doubted Aaron. He didn't think Aaron would be angry or offended to find out he had, though. They were still finding their way, and they were still getting to know each other. James couldn't read Aaron well yet, and the same went for Aaron. Hopefully, that would change soon.

"Are you sure your fathers won't try to convince you to go back?"

"They won't. They know about you and that I'm the one who makes the decisions when it comes to my life. They'll be sad, but they'll understand. What about your parents? Would they try to change your mind if you decided to move?"

James thought about it only for a bit. "They wouldn't. You're right. We're both adults, even though we're young. They'd understand." James grimaced. "And talking about my parents, they want to meet you." They'd been over the moon happy when James had told them he'd met his mate, even though he'd cautioned them that he and Aaron were young and taking things slow. They didn't seem to care, not as long as James was happy, which he was working toward. He didn't know what the future held for him and Aaron, but now that they were together, he couldn't wait to find out.

"That's fine," Aaron said tightly.

James laughed and reached out to take his mate's hand. He raised it to his lips and kissed the knuckles. "You look like I just asked you to throw yourself off a bridge. They won't eat you. I promise."

Aaron shook his head. "I never thought they would."

"You did, and that's fine. I understand why you're nervous. I was nervous, too, when I met your parents, and it didn't even last long. I can stall them if you want, but eventually, they're going to find a way to meet you. It's probably better if you do it on your own terms."

"How did they react when you told them about me?"

That was what Aaron was worried about? "They were happy."

"*What* did you tell them? You mentioned I was a weird shifter?"

James stopped so Aaron could look at him in the eyes when he answered. "You're not a weird shifter. You're incredibly rare and precious."

Aaron's cheeks blazed, and he looked away. "I don't feel precious. I feel like a brat."

James laughed. "Sometimes, you are. That doesn't make you any less precious. And I told them that you were a hybrid and that one of your parents was a harpy shifter while the other is a vampire hunter. I couldn't remember the exact name."

"Krsnik. You mentioned that I could get pregnant?"

Every time James thought about that tidbit of information, he wanted to run away screaming, not because he thought it was weird, but because it was terrifying. Instead of doing that, he swallowed. "I didn't. I figured it was your secret to tell. I know you're not comfortable with it."

Aaron shrugged. "I'm not comfortable with a lot of things. It doesn't mean they don't happen."

"Well, I'm not going to tell them."

"Isn't that going to be awkward when you have to tell them they'll become grandparents?"

James's brain froze. "You want children?" He could hear his voice tremble.

Aaron bit his lower lip. "Eventually, maybe. Not anytime soon, though."

James nodded. He'd never thought about children, but now, he couldn't stop.

Aaron was right. They were nowhere near ready to have kids or even live together, but his future felt brighter and more secure. It was partly thanks to Aaron, but partly, James had finally grown up.

Aaron had half expected James to tell him to fuck off. James knew what he was, and he didn't seem to have a problem with it, but everyone was always hesitant when it came to what his father called his *gift*.

He knew that eventually he would accept it truly was a gift. His fathers were happy to be able to have children, even though the kids were a lot. They wouldn't be having more anytime soon, but they loved the ones they had and how they were born.

Aaron wasn't sure he could ever feel that way, but he supposed things could change. Maybe he was terrified because he was only nineteen and nowhere near ready to have a kid. When he thought about what his father had gone through when he'd first gotten pregnant with him, he started panicking, which wasn't the best thing to do on a date.

So he decided to stop thinking about it. It wouldn't help, and right now, he should focus on James.

James—who was still staring at him as if he wasn't quite sure what to say. Aaron realized he probably shouldn't have pushed or even mentioned that maybe they could have children one day. They probably would have talked about it if he'd been a girl.

"Talking about having children makes me panicky," James admitted.

Aaron laughed, feeling slightly relieved. "Welcome to the club. It makes me feel panicky, too."

"Good to know I'm not the only one. I suppose we should talk about it, though."

"I don't know. We can ignore it. You already know I take birth control, so we don't have to worry about it."

James squeezed Aaron's hand. "We shouldn't ignore it," he said. "It's part of you, and I don't mind. We both know it's a possibility, and it's perfectly fine. We just have to keep it in mind."

Aaron groaned. "I know you're right. I'm just so used to not mentioning it that it's strange to be able to talk about it openly."

"Why are you used to not saying anything about it?"

"Not because my parents don't want me to talk about it or anything like that. It's because I know some people think it's strange, and they're not wrong. It *is* strange."

"Not bad, though."

Aaron stared at James for a few moments before shaking his head. "Not bad." He didn't think it was bad anymore. It might make him strange, but James accepted him the way he was, without asking him to change. He wasn't the only one, either. Aaron's parents accepted him, and so did his friends. Aaron had always felt he was too strange to be loved, but now he knew that wasn't the case. His parents loved him, and it wasn't just because they had to. They loved him because he was Aaron, and because he was their son. They loved him because he was a good person. He wanted to make them proud, and he hoped that eventually, he would.

"We should probably get off the sidewalk," James murmured. "We're kind of blocking the way."

Aaron looked around, noticing that James was right. They *were* blocking the way.

His cheeks felt like they were on fire, but then, he often felt this way when he was with James. He hoped that eventually he would stop feeling embarrassed. James was his mate, and he accepted him with open arms. Aaron should focus on that and nothing else.

They started walking again, and Aaron could feel that James had questions. He might not ask them unless Aaron prodded, but Aaron was wary of doing that. This was supposed to be a date, but instead, it had turned into a conversation about their future. He wasn't sure he was ready to think about that, especially not after talking about the possibility of having their own kids.

"So you're sure you can't get pregnant right now?" James finally asked.

"I'm sure. I even went back to the doctor when I was in Whitedell, just to make sure everything was as it should be. He confirmed that with the birth control, I'm not ovulating."

From James's stare, the words were new to him. He didn't have sisters, but Aaron doubted any of them would talk about ovulating with their brother even if he did. James was going to have to get used to it, though. If he was going to be Aaron's mate and be in his life, he had to know these things.

"Okay. Good."

Aaron couldn't stop himself from laughing. "You look like I hit you on the back of the head. You already knew about this."

"I did, but the conversation we had was kind of vague. You told me you and your father could get pregnant, and that's about it. Now that you've given me more details, it's kind of weird."

The bottom of Aaron's stomach felt like it dropped. "Weird?"

"*You're* not weird," James said. He sounded convinced. "But I can't say I expected this to happen. I never thought I would have to worry about having kids, since I'm gay."

"It's not a worry. It's just something you have to be aware of."

"You're right. And I'm very much aware of the fact that you can get pregnant. I'm sorry. I feel like I'm messing things up."

He wasn't. They needed to have this conversation, and they needed to have it now, before anything happened. James had to know what he was getting himself into, even though telling him about this was terrifying. There was always the fear of being rejected. Aaron had felt this way his entire life, and so far, no one had, or at least, no one important. He hoped that would continue, because he didn't want James to push him away. He especially didn't want James to push him away because of something like this.

This was who Aaron was. He couldn't get rid of this part of himself, and he didn't want to. He'd grown up knowing he could get pregnant and that he was different from everyone else. He was surprisingly fine with it now. When he'd been younger, he'd hated it, but he saw it as the gift it was most of the time now. He knew how happy his parents had been when they'd had children, and that eventually, the same would go for him.

And, hopefully, James.

"What did you have in mind for tonight?" he asked to distract James.

James blinked and smiled. "I'm not really sure. I didn't have time to organize anything. Maybe we can just get dinner or something like that?"

"Is that why you were asking if I was taking birth control? Because you want to have dinner?"

James's cheeks blazed, very much like Aaron's felt, and Aaron laughed. It was good to know he wasn't the only one fumbling through their relationship.

"I had nothing specific in mind. It was just a question. But we already had sex once, and we both know it's going to happen again. I wanted to be sure we have everything under control. I don't care that you can have children, but I don't want you to get pregnant by surprise."

"You're right. You did the right thing asking me about it." Aaron was glad it wasn't a secret or something they needed to avoid talking about. He'd always expected it to be once he found someone to be with, but he'd been lucky enough to meet his mate and that James truly didn't care.

"Actually, I have a question," James said.

Aaron swallowed, suddenly nervous. "What is it?"

"I saw your harpy form from a distance before. I was kind of curious and wondering if I could see it from up close?"

Aaron was relieved and couldn't stop smiling. "A lot of people are curious about my harpy form, and of course you can see it from up close." He looked around. "I don't think that doing it in the middle of town is the best idea, though."

James grinned. "I never thought it was. We can go to pack territory."

"Do you have a place in mind?"

"I do. My parents are out for the evening, and so is my younger brother. We have the house to ourselves."

Aaron blinked. He hadn't expected that, and he wasn't quite sure what to make of it. "What are you saying?"

James rolled his eyes. "I'm not trying to get you into bed,

not if you don't want that. I just wanted you to know it was a possibility."

Suddenly, Aaron was nervous. He and James had had sex, but it had been in a car, and James hadn't been able to see him well. Now he would, because Aaron had no doubt that the evening would end with them in James's bed.

James knew what to expect, at least in part. He'd seen Aaron's harpy form from a distance before, but he was pretty sure it was very different from up close, especially knowing what he did now. Aaron's harpy form wasn't just an exterior change. It came with his ability to become pregnant and have children, which made James wonder if he'd ever had a problem with it. Knowing Aaron, he wouldn't be surprised if his mate had refused to shift into his harpy form when he was younger.

That was in the past, though. Aaron seemed all too happy to shift now that they were in pack territory.

They were outside at James's house. Like he'd promised, his parents weren't there, and neither was his brother. His parents were on a date tonight, and his mom had made sure to tell him they would be spending the night in a hotel. James hadn't wanted to hear anything about that, and especially not that it meant he would have the house to himself and that he could invite anyone he wanted. His brother Kendall was out, too, all too happy to be able to spend time away from his family.

That meant the house was empty and would be the entire night.

It made James nervous. The one time they'd had sex, it had felt good. He couldn't wait to do it again, but he also couldn't stop thinking about the consequences it could have.

Maybe he should stop. He and Aaron had agreed they

weren't ready to have children or even to start thinking about it. Aaron was convinced it wouldn't happen, and James needed to forget about it, at least for now. He should focus on Aaron, not on what could or couldn't happen.

"Where are we doing this?" Aaron asked, looking around. He was obviously curious about James's house.

James would be more than happy to show him around. "Wherever you want. We don't have close neighbors, so no one's going to see you, if that's what you're asking."

"It wasn't, but good to know. I can just shift, then? You're sure no one is going to walk in on us?"

"No one should, no. My parents are away for the night, and so is my brother. My other brother lives in town and doesn't have a reason to be here, and none of our neighbors will be able to see you, even if you fly. They wouldn't know what to look for anyway."

Aaron slowly nodded. He looked around one last time, then took off his jacket and shirt.

James took a moment to stare at his mate. He truly was gorgeous, and now that James could see him well, he was delighted to find out that the freckles weren't just on Aaron's face. They peppered his entire body, or at least, he hoped so. It certainly looked like it from here. As corny as it was, he kind of wanted to lick every single one of them.

Aaron handed James his shirt and jacket, and James took them. He held them close to his body, unable to look away.

He thought he knew what to expect. He was aware that Aaron was much bigger when he shifted into his harpy form.

James still wasn't prepared for what he saw once it happened.

Aaron was glorious. He was tall even in his human form, but he was almost seven feet tall once he shifted. It was kind of intimidating, even knowing Aaron would never hurt him. His torso wasn't the only thing that looked gorgeous. His wings were enormous, and they were a bronze color that reflected the dying rays of the sun.

Aaron squared his shoulders, and their gazes locked. James knew that Aaron expected to be rejected, and he wanted his mate to know that was never going to happen. How could he reject Aaron for something he was and couldn't change? "You're gorgeous," he said.

Aaron grinned, exposing his fangs. "You're sure about that?"

"More than sure."

Aaron raised his hands, and James swallowed at the sight of the claws that tipped his fingers. Aaron also had black eyes, and while James instantly missed the violet eyes he usually had, he loved these, too.

He held out his hand.

Aaron blinked at it and hesitated. He clearly hadn't expected James to be okay with this. James needed him to know he was. When Aaron didn't reach out to him, he put the jacket and shirt he was still holding into his car, closed the door, and stepped closer to Aaron. As Aaron watched him, he wrapped his arms around him and pressed himself against his mate's body.

It was odd. It was like nothing James knew, but it didn't matter. It was still Aaron, and James still loved it.

Aaron finally wrapped his arms around James, and they stood hugging each other. When James tilted his head up, Aaron looked hesitant. James had to hook both his arms around his mate's neck and pull him down to be able to kiss him. "The only problem I have with this is that you're way too tall for me when you're in this form," he grumbled.

Aaron laughed and tightened his hold on James. "I'm sorry."

"Don't be. We might have to invest in a ladder or something like that, though."

"You truly don't care?"

"Why would I care? No matter how you look, you're still Aaron, and that's all that matters." James slid a hand toward the wings on Aaron's back. He gently touched the bronze feathers, watching them tremble and shiver under his fingers. "Is this okay?" he murmured.

Aaron nodded, then kissed James again.

James was more than happy to kiss his mate back, or at least, he was until he felt his feet leave the ground. His eyes opened wide, and he looked around. "What are you doing?" he asked.

"Do you trust me?"

"Of course I do." James didn't even have to think about it.

Aaron nodded. "I won't let you fall. I promise. I can still go back down if you need me to, though."

James didn't want to go back down. "Make me fly," he told Aaron.

Aaron obeyed.

It was exhilarating, once James got over the initial fear. He was pressed against his mate, and he wasn't afraid of falling. He put his cheek against Aaron's chest, his eyes burning with the wind. He didn't close them, though. He looked at pack territory under them, and even though Aaron didn't go far or too high, it still felt precious. It was something he and Aaron would share, something only they would know about. James doubted Aaron had ever taken anyone else flying, and it made him feel special.

And he was. He was Aaron's mate, and now that Aaron had gotten over the shock and fear, they were both ready to work toward their future.

James pointed at a window at the house. "That's my bedroom. I can open the window from outside."

Aaron's chest rumbled with laughter. "Are you telling me something?"

"Only that it's my window. Do what you want with that knowledge."

Aaron laughed again. James was pretty sure the sound was happier than he'd ever heard it coming from his mate. This had been the last hurdle between them. Aaron had been terrified James would reject him and his harpy form, but James had known he wouldn't. Now, they were both convinced of it.

He wasn't surprised when Aaron flew toward the window. They both knew what was going to happen, and James didn't want to stop it.

They were nowhere ready to bond, but that didn't mean they couldn't make love.

Aaron landed on the roof. He kept his hands on James as James pushed open his bedroom window. James used to sneak out when he was a teenager—he was pretty sure his parents had known about it but had ignored it since he stayed in pack territory—so he knew exactly where to put his feet so he wouldn't tumble down.

Aaron never stopped touching James as James scrambled through the window. He hadn't expected their date to end this way, so he rushed around the room, picking up dirty clothes and shoving things under the bed. He heard Aaron chuckle behind him, and he snapped into a standing position, his cheeks on fire. "Sorry. I didn't expect you to come around today."

Aaron looked around the room. "It's not as bad as mine. Don't worry about it."

James wished he'd at least changed the sheets. He eyed the bed, but it was too late for that, so he didn't even try. He should have made it this morning, dammit.

They both stood still. After a few minutes, Aaron shifted back into his human form. As much as James found the harpy form gorgeous, he preferred Aaron's human form. It was familiar and didn't make him feel intimidated or like Aaron could have better. He couldn't. James was his mate, and that was that.

James shuffled his feet. "What do you want to do? We could watch a movie."

Aaron arched a brow. "Is that really why you asked me to come and told me the house would be empty the rest of the night?"

James had never been a blusher, but it seemed like Aaron had changed that, which he wasn't particularly happy about. "I don't expect anything, if that's what you're asking."

Aaron moved closer. "It's not. I'm asking what you *want*."

James sucked in a breath. "To be with you."

"You are. And we can watch a movie if you want."

James grinned. "But?"

"But I don't want to watch a movie." Aaron reached for James, hooking his arm around James's waist and pulling him closer.

James pressed both hands against Aaron's naked chest. Aaron's skin was chilly from the flight, but it warmed under his palms even as Aaron shivered. James was pretty sure the cold had nothing to do with that, though.

He slid his palms up and down, then leaned closer and kissed the spot just above Aaron's heart. He continued pressing his lips to Aaron's skin, moving down until he got to a nipple. He flicked his tongue out, grinning at the shudder that ran through Aaron's body.

"No movie, then?" Aaron asked in a rough voice.

"No movie." Unless it was porn, but now wasn't the right moment to bring that up.

James kissed Aaron. He wanted to give his mate the world, and he hoped he would make Aaron happy.

He was certainly going to try.

Aaron kissed back. His hands slid down James's hips to his

ass, which made him smile. It was as if he couldn't stop when he was with Aaron. He knew that eventually, they would get used to being together, but everything was new and exciting, and James wanted more. He stroked his hands down to Aaron's waist and played with the button of his jeans for a moment, but not too long. He could feel Aaron was hard, and so was he.

He unfastened Aaron's jeans and pushed his hands inside, parting the fabric to get to Aaron's cock. Aaron sucked in a breath. James ran his fingertips on every inch of skin he could get to, and that seemed to snap Aaron into action. He pushed James's jacket off his shoulders, and James had to let go so he could get rid of it. He didn't want to be interrupted again, so he took off his hoodie and sweater, too, and dumped everything on the floor.

He pressed his chest against Aaron's, sighing at the touch of skin against skin. This was what he wanted, and from the looks of it, so did Aaron.

Aaron pushed, and they stumbled back. James yelped when his legs hit something, but Aaron was holding him—until he wasn't. Aaron grinned and let go. James bounced on the mattress, glaring at his mate but more than happy to open his arms so that Aaron could climb into them. Aaron didn't, though. Instead, he pulled James's shoes and socks off, then his jeans. James scrambled to undo them, and when they slid down his legs, he pushed his underwear along with them.

Then he was naked. He swallowed, hoping Aaron liked what he was seeing. He didn't seem to hate it, which James supposed was a relief. He wasn't overly worried, though, especially not when Aaron got rid of his jeans, too, and James saw he was still hard.

Aaron climbed onto the bed. James wanted him closer, but Aaron stopped at James's groin, kissing his stomach and upper thighs—everywhere but where James wanted him to.

James didn't say anything, though. He could see in the tilt of Aaron's smile that he was doing it on purpose. Instead of protesting, he reached for the pillow he never slept on, and pushed his hand under it as Aaron breathed against the head of his cock. James screwed his eyes shut and tried to focus on what he was doing, which was getting the lube out. He smacked it against Aaron's arm, getting his attention and ending the torture.

Aaron blinked at it as if he'd never seen a bottle of lube. "What?"

"We're going to need that."

Aaron nodded, still staring. "I—how do you want me?"

James stretched, grinning at the way Aaron moved his focus from the lube to his body. "I thought we could stay this way."

Aaron nodded and moved to the side, and James realized what he was doing. "That's not what I meant," he protested.

"Don't you want to fuck me?"

"Of course I do. But right now, I want you to fuck me more."

Aaron's eyes were wide and his cheeks flushed. "Yeah? Guys usually want to fuck me."

"Well, I'm not *guys*, and while I do want that, it can wait." James wiggled his eyebrows. "We have the entire night, remember?"

Aaron grinned. "We do." He grabbed the lube. "Don't worry—I know what to do."

"That's what I was hoping." James opened his legs to give Aaron space to do what he needed to do.

Aaron didn't seem to want to rush things, though. He went down to his stomach and slicked his fingers, then put both his hands and his mouth to work—and this time, it was exactly where James wanted it.

James buried his fingers into Aaron's red hair, gently

pulling and smiling at Aaron's groans. Even though Aaron was going to fuck him, it didn't mean James had to lie there doing nothing. Besides, it didn't take long for James to need Aaron to stop doing what he was doing. He wouldn't mind coming in Aaron's mouth, but he wanted Aaron's body on his. He wanted to be able to hug his mate, to wrap himself around Aaron as Aaron moved inside of him, to feel like they were one. Right now, it was tempting to say fuck it and decide to bond, but James knew they would both regret it come morning. They couldn't bond now, but it didn't mean they couldn't be as close as possible.

James pulled harder on Aaron's hair until Aaron let go and looked up. He had three fingers in James's ass, and his mouth was slick. "What?"

"Come here," James murmured.

"I don't know if you're ready."

"I am. We'll take things slow." James was touched at how much Aaron cared, although not surprised. "I need you up here."

Aaron stared for a moment before nodding and finally moving.

Aaron didn't want to hurt James, but he had to trust him. James knew his body best, and if he wanted this to happen now, Aaron wasn't going to protest. If it was up to him, they would already be done. He felt like his cock was going to explode, but now would be too soon. He needed to get inside James first.

All of the other guys Aaron had slept with—which weren't that many—had insisted they fuck Aaron. He hadn't minded much, because he enjoyed it, but he couldn't deny he wanted to do this more. Getting fucked always made him nervous because of the pregnancy risk, even with condoms and his birth control.

Today was different. Even when James fucked Aaron later, it would be different because Aaron knew that if something happened and both the condom and his pills failed, he wouldn't be left alone. No matter what happened, James would be right next to him, whether they were ready or not. They were a team against the world, whatever it threw at them.

And that, more than anything, made Aaron okay with it.

James wrapped his legs around Aaron's hips as Aaron moved into place. Aaron was nervous, even though he knew he had no reason to be. James would accept him whatever happened, even if this ended up being a disaster.

It wasn't. Aaron fumbled a bit trying to get his cock against James's hole, and he had to push harder than he'd expected to get inside of him, but once he did, he forgot about everything that wasn't James and how he felt around him. It was hard not to come right away, but Aaron wanted James to enjoy this as much as he did. He wanted them to do it together.

It was overwhelming in the best of ways. James hugged Aaron and whispered to him the entire time, making him feel grounded and loved. He'd been an idiot to think he wasn't and that he had to stay away from James.

All of that was over now, and Aaron focused on what he and James were. It was hard to avoid looking at James's neck, especially when James was all flushed and sweaty, so Aaron kissed James. That way, neither of them would be tempted to do something stupid.

James pushed a hand between their bodies, seeking his cock. Aaron sucked in his stomach to give him space, then realized he should be the one doing James's cock. He rose on one arm and tried to grab it with the other while still kissing James, and they both laughed when it proved impossible to coordinate all of that. James batted Aaron's hand away, clearly wanting to do it on his own, which was more than fine with Aaron.

They clung to each other as they moved. James made little sounds that thrilled Aaron and pushed him closer and closer to orgasm. It was a mix of everything – the scents of their bodies pressed together, the sounds James made, knowing James was going to sleep in this bed night after night and that eventually, they would become one. Aaron was in love with James, and he couldn't wait to see what was next with him, how they would build a life together.

He screwed his eyes shut when he came and made sure to avoid James's neck. James dug the nails of his free hand into Aaron's shoulder, but Aaron didn't care about the flash of pain. He only cared that he was coming inside his mate and that James was right there with him, whimpering and pressing as close as he could to Aaron. Aaron held him close and rolled them to their side so they could cuddle.

"We should think about eating eventually," James murmured.

"That's what you're thinking about after what just happened?"

James chuckled. "What? You made me hungry."

"Then I'll feed you." Today and every day from now on.

Chapter Seven

Aaron was nervous. He was convinced about what he was doing, but that didn't mean it wasn't a huge change for him.

"You can still change your mind," his father said, gently touching his knee.

Aaron stared at the form in front of him and shook his head. "I can do it. I *want* to do it."

"I know. You can take your time making decisions, though. We'll support you either way."

Aaron sucked in a breath, grabbed the pen on the desk next to the form, and used it to sign at the bottom of it quickly. Once he'd done it, he felt lighter and just as happy as he'd been before.

He dropped the pen and leaned back in his chair. Bran was sitting on the other side of the desk, and he nodded, obviously pleased. "Good. Welcome to the enforcers, Aaron," he said.

Aaron beamed. "Thank you."

"I hope you won't regret this decision, but if you do, come to me. We can talk about it."

"I don't think I'll regret it."

"Even though you won't be working with your team anymore?"

Okay, so maybe that was one thing Aaron would regret. He'd come to like the entire team, and he would miss them. He would see them again, though. They all lived in Gillham, and now, so did he. "It'll be fine. I knew it was temporary, and they showed me how much I would love this job."

"All right. You know what's next. I hope you're ready."

Aaron wasn't sure he was, but this was one thing he wasn't running away from. Tomorrow, he was starting training, and even though he knew it was going to be hard, he couldn't wait. Once training was over, he would be assigned to a team, and he hoped he would fit in with them as well as he had with the team he'd shadowed.

He and his fathers got to their feet to leave the office. Aaron opened the door, stumbling when he saw the entire team was there. They stared at him until he smiled and raised his thumb up, and when he did, they cheered.

Lorcan slapped Aaron on the back. "I knew you would do it."

"It's thanks to you guys."

"Nah. We didn't do anything. That was all you, and we're proud of you, kid."

Aaron wasn't even offended by the *kid* part. He truly was a kid next to the team, but now, he realized it wasn't a bad thing.

It wasn't a bad thing that he was young and that he had a lot to learn, or that he wasn't ready for some things. He had time.

The team parted, and Aaron noticed James was there, too. He swallowed but couldn't stop smiling.

He and his mate were closer than ever. They still hadn't talked about bonding, and Aaron didn't think it would happen anytime soon, but he knew that eventually, they would. There was no way around it, not when he was falling in love with James.

James had supported him through all of this. He'd given Aaron time and space, and he'd welcomed him into his life, even though Aaron had been an asshole in the beginning. They were going strong now, and Aaron knew they would continue doing so.

They weren't moving in together yet, since Aaron was going to spend more time in the enforcers' building training and things like that, but it was on the horizon, and for once, Aaron couldn't wait. He was nervous, but he'd come to understand that being nervous about your future and not knowing what would happen wasn't a bad thing. It was what everyone went through, and Aaron wasn't special, not that way.

He had no idea what the future held, but he was so much more confident, both in himself and in the world. He had a job, a loving family, parents who had tried their best to help him and show him that he was loved, and his mate. No matter what happened, he would always have those two last things, and he knew they would get him through hard times. Even if he decided that being an enforcer wasn't for him, they would be there.

He suspected he would love being an enforcer, though. He had when he'd been working with Sue and her team, and although that would change now that he truly was an enforcer, it wouldn't be enough to make him change his mind.

"Ready for lunch?" Troy asked, wrapping an arm around Aaron's shoulders.

Aaron nodded and held his hand out to James, who came without hesitating.

It was still awkward for them to be with each other's parents, but they were dealing with that, too. No one had tried to dissuade them from being together or to convince them to slow things down. They knew it wasn't their relationship or their business, and even though they were happy, they stayed out of it. Still, James was nervous, and Aaron pulled him closer, kissing his temple. "You know they love you," he murmured.

"That doesn't make it any easier."

Aaron chuckled. "It should. They're not going to interrogate you about what your plans are for me or anything like that. They know that what we do is our business, and only ours."

James peeked around Aaron to look at Aaron's dads. They were talking with a few of the enforcers, not paying attention to Aaron and James.

Or at least, that was what they were trying to act like. Aaron was pretty sure his dads were watching them, but that was because they wanted to make sure Aaron was okay. It was never going to change. He was their son, and even when he was fifty, he would still be. He didn't mind it, though.

They knew when to keep their distance and when to push for Aaron to talk to them, and now that Aaron had realized how stupid he'd been, their relationship was healing. He supposed that the fact that he'd moved away also helped. He missed his parents and his siblings, and it was easier to spend time with them when he could.

"Where are the kids today?" James asked.

"At home. Nysys is babysitting them, even though he wanted to be here."

"I can't wait to meet him."

"The same goes for him." But Aaron was more than happy to keep those two away from each other, at least for a bit. Nysys would have hundreds of questions for James, and James would be overwhelmed. James wasn't going to leave Aaron for that, but meeting his parents was already overwhelming enough as it was.

Once they were out of the enforcers' building, Aaron took a deep breath and closed his eyes. The sun warmed his face, and he held James tighter.

This was his life now. He was an enforcer, and he had a family and a mate. He wasn't lost anymore, and he knew he wasn't a freak. He was loved, which in the end, was all that mattered.

YOU MAY ALSO ENJOY THE FOLLOWING FROM eXTASY BOOKS INC:

Rise from the Ashes
Catherine Lievens

Excerpt

Reece stumbled home. He couldn't remember a time when he'd been so angry and disappointed, even though he shouldn't be. He shouldn't feel this way. He wasn't allowed to, and that was his own fault.

He was the one who'd always kept Sage at arm's length. He was the one who'd ignored all the times Sage tried to get closer. He'd also ignored the signs that Sage felt more than friendship for him, and this was the result.

And he knew it was better this way.

Carey was Sage's mate. He and Sage belong together, and Reece didn't have a say in that, no matter how angry he was. He shouldn't be, though. He'd had plenty of occasions to be with Sage. He and Sage could have been together almost since the beginning, when Sage first arrived. But instead, Reece had made sure they were only friends.

And now he'd lost Sage forever.

He slammed his front door shut and leaned against it, closing his eyes and trying to breathe through the anger and the pain.

He knew it was better that way, and not only because Carey and Sage were mates. It was better because of his own past. It was better because he couldn't fall in love again. He couldn't let that happen, not the way it had happened before. He wouldn't be able to stand a loss of that entity again, and that was why he'd ignored Sage's shy openings.

He wasn't sure he could watch Sage one of with Carey though.

Eventually, it would happen. Reece could imagine how things would go—Sage would try talking to him at least a few times, possibly more. He would try to explain what had happened with Carey, and he would apologize. That was just how Sage was. He always apologized, even when he didn't have anything to apologize for.

So he would try to make Reece see that if Reece wanted, he could ignore the bond he shared with Carey. Reece was almost a hundred percent sure that would happen, and Reece would tell him that it didn't matter, that he should focus on Carey because Carey was his mate and they belonged together. Sage wouldn't push. He never did. That was why he and Reece were still only friends. Everyone knew there was more than that between them, or at least, that there had been. That was over now, though.

Everything was over.

Reece didn't want to have to watch Sage and Carey be happy together. The instinct to pack and leave was strong. He might have if the pack hadn't been his home.

But it was.

Reece's past had shown him that, and he knew things wouldn't go well if he left, no matter how much he wanted to. He would have to face the pain and deal with it. He was used to doing that anyway. This wouldn't any different.

A knock on the front door made him jump. He didn't want to talk to whoever was on the other side of it, even though there was a strong possibility that someone was Sage. Reece decided to ignore it and stayed as still as he could, but he should have known better.

"I know you're in there," Frederic said.

Reece should have known Frederic would come by. He was Reece's best friend, and more than once, he'd asked Reece why he didn't talk to Sage, why the two of them weren't together. He didn't know what Reece had gone through and why he couldn't have anything with Sage or anyone else ever again.

"I saw you walk home. Why aren't you at the party? What happened with Sage and Carey? I saw the three of you talk, then you left, and you looked angry. Did Carey say something?"

Reece knew Frederic wasn't going anywhere. Until Reece opened his door, he would stay there, flinging questions and waiting for answers. Not getting them wasn't going to deter him. It never did.

Reece sighed heavily, then pushed away from the door and opened it. He glared at Frederic, but Frederic ignored him. He already had more questions. "Was Carey rude to you? Because from what I know, he's not a bad guy, just weird. You probably shouldn't be offended by whatever he told you, but it was that bad, you need to talk to him, or better yet, Camden. He'll tell Carey to shut the fuck up or something like that."

Reece crossed his arms over his chest. "Why do you think he was rude to me?"

Frederic arched a brow. "Remember that bit about you stomping away looking angry? That's why."

Reece needed to make a decision. He could tell Frederic what had happened, or he could act as if everything was fine. He doubted Frederic would believe him, but maybe he wouldn't push.

Hope was the last thing to die and all that.

Reece shook his head and took a step back so Frederic could come in. "You should go back to the party," he said.

"I'm not going back until you talk to me. I've had enough

of this island bullshit. Since you came back, you've isolated yourself even more, and I don't like it. It's been years, Reece. Talk to me. Please."

Reece couldn't. He'd been back seven years, and he'd kept the pain and memories close to his heart. He didn't want that to change. He couldn't allow that to happen because it would make his daily life close to impossible to live. He needed to be able to ignore what had happened to go on.

"Nothing happened with Carey and me. He came close, told Sage they're mates, and that was that."

Frederic blinked. "They're mates?"

"Looks like it. Sage confirmed it, and I believe him."

Frederic's expression softened. "But you and Sage have something, right?"

Reece knew everyone had noticed. That didn't mean he was comfortable with it, or that he was going to confirm that he and Sage had been dancing around each other. "We're friends. That's all."

"You know it's more than that. We all do."

"We're friends," Reece repeated. He needed Frederic to stop pushing. He didn't want to break in front of his best friend, and that was what would happen if Frederic continued asking questions.

"I see you don't want to talk about that. That's fine."

Reece could have kissed Frederic for finally getting the hint. "You should go back to the party."

Frederic peered at Reece, and Reece held his breath. He needed some time alone. He already knew that the memories would come back, as strong as if everything was happening all over again. He needed to be alone to go through that. When he broke down, he wanted no one to see it, not even his best friend.

"I'm going, I'm going. I'm just worried about you, and so is everyone else," Frederic said. His voice was softer, and Reece suspected he felt sorry for him. Reece hated that, but he couldn't bring himself to care much, not when the memories were already flooding his mind. He always had a hard time ignoring them when this kind of thing happened, and Carey had never definitely triggered something. "I'll be fine," he insisted.

"Maybe. Maybe not. I don't think even you know. But I'm here if you need anything, even if it's only to talk. You're my best friend, even though we were away from each other for years. That hasn't changed, and it never will, even though you're so very different since you came back. I'm here for you, whatever you need. And I'm not the only one."

Reece knew that. That was the only reason he was still here with the pack. It would have been easier for him to start a new life somewhere else, somewhere no one knew him, but this was good, too. No one in the pack knew about his mate and their son. No one in the pack knew Reece had lost both of them. That meant they didn't ask questions, but they were there for Reece when he needed them.

Now wasn't one of those moments. The only thing Reece needed was to be alone, and he was grateful to see Frederic's back as he left.

About the Author

Catherine is the creator of several series, most of them paranormal, including the Whitedell Pride Series and the Gillham Pack Series. While she graduated in translation, she decided to go the writer's way because it was more fun to create her own stories and characters.

She's been living in Italy for more than twenty years, but she's a daughter of the North—Belgium to be precise—and she misses it so much that she's already planning to move back.

She loves pizza—probably too much —her son, her pets, and of course, books. She sneaks some reading time into her schedule every time she has five minutes free from writing, demands from her various pets and son, and lastly, housework.

Connect with her:

lievens.catherine@gmail.com
BookBub: https://www.bookbub.com/authors/catherine-lievens
Website: https://authorcatherinelievens.com/
Facebook: https://www.facebook.com/catherine.lievens.9
Facebook Group: https://www.facebook.com/groups/411788002341528/
Twitter: https://twitter.com/authorCLievens
Newsletter: http://eepurl.com/c-uvKn

www.ingramcontent.com/pod-product-compliance
Lightning Source LLC
LaVergne TN
LVHW020638100826
845148LV00012B/2231
* 9 7 8 1 4 8 7 4 3 1 7 6 1 *